This is Meant to Be

Wild Child Reckless Book Two

Juliet McKinley

Suddenly Juliet

To everyone who has supported me while I chase this dream.

To everyone who hasn't supported me while I chase this dream.

I'm still chasing anyway.

xx

Prologue

Jensen

As they lower the coffin, I try to feel something other than relief, but I can't. After living with Mom for twelve years, I've realized through therapy that she was a narcissist, incapable of loving me as I needed. It's her failing, not mine. I shouldn't hold myself to her impossible standards.

There are a few people here from Thompson Ritchers, where Mom was CFO, but I doubt they're grieving. Dad stands beside me while the priest speaks about Mary Elizabeth Parker—intelligent, beautiful, and successful, from a prominent Savannah family, Oxford and Stanford educated, and married to Michael, a chef. Despite her accomplishments, the truth was different: Mom was unfaithful, and her death came after another reckless night.

My grandparents sit across from us, stoic and fake, believing Dad and I will move in with them. They have no idea we're heading straight to California, leaving Savannah behind. Eventually, we'll head to Texas and Dad's family, but we're just getting as far from them as possible now. The only good thing

Mom did was make me her beneficiary, but I have plans. Music is my future, not her money.

The funeral ends, and my grandparents approach, reeking of Chanel and scotch, trying to act like we're a loving family. I step back, refusing to play along. They talk about the wake and expect me to show up in their world, but they don't know I'm done with Vanguard Prep and their control. When Mom died, he knew they would start meddling, so we packed up and planned our escape.

Dad squeezes my hand as we leave the cemetery, and I know our future isn't here—it's in Texas.

Chapter One

Jensen- One Year Later

The Parker family is loud and boisterous, the house is warm and inviting, and the furniture is soft and plump with stuffing, well worn.

"Well, we're not in Kansas anymore," I whisper to my dad before being enveloped in a crushing hug.

"Jensen, *mijo*! You're here! Ah, *pobresito*, so skinny." She turns and spits out rapid-fire Spanish, and a family member behind her turns to the kitchen.

"Come in, come in! It is so good to see you! We have missed you so much!" I am passed around from family member to family member, receiving hugs and the occasional kiss before I find myself at the table, breathless, my back killing me, and a plate of something I don't recognize in front of me.

"Um, I'm not hungry at the moment. Dad and I stopped and got lunch just a few hours ago." I poke at the items on the plate with a fork.

"What is the matter? Have you never had a tamale before?" Abuela turns to Dad, and they argue back and forth in Spanish.

"Oh. Sorry. No. Mother would have had a fit if the cooks had served this food at the house." At the mention of my mother, Abuela crosses herself and then spits on the floor. I can guess the significance. She's not wrong. Someone sits down next to me, takes a tamale, and shows me how to unwrap it. I take a tentative bite before scarfing the whole thing. Man, these are good. I'm on my third when the front door opens, and in walks someone I've yet to meet. Her red hair is in a riot of curls around her head, and her denim shorts are frayed.

"One of these does not belong. One of these is not like the others," I murmur, and the guy sitting next to me, Cousin Vincent, I think, chuckles.

"You have no idea."

"Abuela Parker! It's Delilah! I am here to pick up my order! Hey! Who does the guitar belong to? Gilberto! Did you finally listen to me and start playing?" She's walking through the house, chatting and laughing with my family like she's always belonged, but when she picks up my guitar, I stand up sharply; the scrape of the chair against the floor cuts through the chatter.

"That's mine. Please do not touch it." When she turns and faces me, I am met with large green eyes and freckles that only highlight her eyes and nose. When she smiles, I immediately smile back, but a piece of tamale goes down the wrong pipe, and I start coughing and choking. When she laughs, I pick up my water glass to regain control.

"Delilah! *Mija*! I have your order right here. Now I know you like the chicken and cream cheese. So, I gave you an extra dozen. Don't tell your brother. He will eat them all, and then I must take measures. I also slipped you some pan de polvo in there." She thrusts a massive box at Delilah before beaming at me. My grandmother tucks around Delilah like a daughter. "*Mijo*, come meet Delilah! You will like her, she's a musician as well. Quiet the voice on this one." She nudges Delilah, who blushes. "She is going to make our city proud one day!"

"Jensen?! Do you mean he finally showed up?! How exciting!" She wraps her arms around my waist, hugging me. The top of her head barely comes to my shoulders and smells like flowers, but I can't place which ones. When the hug continues longer than what I'm used to, I clear my throat, and she jumps back.

"Sorry. Abuela told me you were coming, but I didn't realize you had arrived. You play?"

"Yeah. I play. I'm guessing you do as well?"

"I'm mostly alone, but I have considered starting a band. Do you want to play together sometime? I'm available after school unless you are going to work."

I glance back at my dad, and he shakes his head no.

"Looks like I am free after school. Do you wanna go play now?"

"I have to take these tamales home, but I can afterward. You can come with me now if you want. Mom's at work, and James is usually off doing Lord knows what, so it's just me."

I grab my bag and sling my guitar onto my back. "Dad, I'll be back later?" I phrase it as a question, but I see him smiling.

"That's fine, *mijo*, have fun. Be home in time for dinner."

The screen door slaps closed behind me as we make our way down the steps.

"So you lived in Georgia and California, huh? That sounds fun. I've never lived anywhere other than here." Delilah keeps up a steady stream of chatter while walking to her house. I answer when I can, but for the most part, I use this time to get a good look at the town I will call home for the next five years. People greet each other on the street, and many ask Delilah about her mom or brother, who I learned is the James she mentioned earlier. She answers everyone cheerfully and seems generally liked by everyone. The very notion shocks me. I couldn't have called any of my neighbors before by name, much less picked them out of a lineup. We walk up to a house that resembles many others in this town, with whiteboards, oversized windows, and a wraparound porch. Delilah bounds up the steps, hollering for James as she opens the door. When no one answers, she motions me into the house.

"James is out still, I guess. Head on down the hall. My room is at the first door on the right. I will put these tamales up, and I'll be there." She heads toward what I assume is the kitchen, and I make my way down the hall. Family pictures line the halls. A young woman next to a man in army greens, his red hair shining in the sun. The same young woman in a man's leather jacket sitting on a front porch glider, grinning at the camera. The young man with a bag at his feet, other men in uniform around him, blowing a kiss at the camera. The same couple is holding a baby boy; further down the hall, the boy is older, and another baby, Delilah, I assume, joins the pictures. As I walk further down, the man stops appearing in the photographs. I walk back to get to the last photo of him. Delilah is held high in one arm, and her brother hangs off the other. They are all laughing. I stand there staring at that photograph.

"He was in the Army. A Ranger. He went on a mission but never made it back." Delilah's voice is quiet, and I turn to look at her, but she isn't looking at me; she's staring at that picture. Her voice is far away when she continues, trapped in a memory. "That was the year X moved in next door. Dad got called back in; he was supposed to retire, but they begged him to take this last mission. I can still hear his voice at night and smell him. I think the worst part of losing someone you love is the memories. Abuela told me you lost your mom, so you know what I mean."

I give her a sad smile and shake my head. "No, I don't know what you mean. Honestly, I was glad when my mom died. She was a horrible person who made mine and my dad's lives hell for years. She deserves every bit of the pain she inflicted on us and then some. Long may she rot." I look up from my shoes, where my gaze had dropped, to see Delilah's shocked face. I rub the back of my neck in embarrassment. "I'm sorry I—oomph." Delilah launches herself at me and hugs me tight.

"I am so sorry you had to go through that. I am so sorry your mom didn't love you as you should have been loved. She didn't deserve you or your dad. I promise from now on, you'll always have me." I slowly hug her back. After several moments, we step apart, and I watch as Delilah wipes her eyes before chuckling.

"That is not what we are supposed to be doing! Enough sappy stuff! Let's play!"

"Let's play," I agree, hugging her close to my side.

Three hours later, I am in awe of Delilah and her voice. I can easily understand why she is so widely popular. She has the girl next door look combined with a voice that makes you think of starry Texas nights and crackling bonfires. I just know she's going to go far, and I decide then and there that I want to be with her.

Chapter Two

Lily- Two Years Later

"Your father requests your presence."

I look up and see Adrian standing in my doorway. He's my father's goon and built like a brick shit house. The skin showing around his suit is scarred and covered in tattoos. Frankly, he scares the shit out of me, but I can't let him know that.

"You don't knock?" I make my tone as bratty as possible. The last thing I want is to go to my father's office, but delaying will only anger him more. Since my mom left last year, his temper has been more and more unpredictable.

"I don't knock. Your father expects you now." He gives me a look before turning and walking away.

As I sigh, I put my pen on my English paper and then follow him down the hall. I check my prep school uniform skirt, and it is smooth as we reach the mahogany double doors. I used to love these doors as they were big and shiny, and meant I was about to see my favorite person, Father. I was a hardcore daddy's girl. But then he became governor, and things changed. The father I knew was replaced by a stranger. Family holidays became scripted, family dinners became catered parties with rail-thin women wearing Chanel and men drinking brandy while smoking cigars. Soon after, I couldn't even recognize my life anymore.

I knock on the door and wait, my eyes fixed on my sneakers.

"Enter."

I open the door and walk in, standing before his desk. The office is filled with the smell of his cologne and cigars—a sign that he must have had a meeting earlier. Colton Henry DuPont III stands behind his desk, a sheaf of papers in his right hand and a tumbler of scotch in his left. He sits the pieces of writing down and takes a deep sip of his drink before sitting down.

"You called for me, Father?"

"I did. I just got off the phone with your math professor. You've got a B in Advanced Algebra?"

I suck in a breath, realizing that I haven't been doing as well as I could have. I foolishly thought I had more time to improve before my teacher informed my father. But every teacher at school is either in awe of or terrified of him. I should have known Father would be told the minute my grade dipped below an A.

"Yes, sir."

"What am I going to do with you, Lillian Rose? How can I possibly put you up for acceptance at Wellesley if my own daughter is an idiot?!" He roars the word idiot, stands up, and slams his fist on his desk.

I jump in surprise as his fist makes contact with the wood of his desk. He's not in a good mood today, but that's not surprising; his good moods are generally reserved for when Clarissa or the press are around. Just then, the door swings open, and the devil herself walks in.

"Donny, darling, I just wanted to talk to you about the wedding—" Clarissa breaks off as she notices me, her nose wrinkling as if she smells something funny. Watching Clarissa try to hide her disdain is my lightbulb moment. The last time I brought up going to stay with Mom, it was shut down. Almost violently. However, this could be a situation I could use to my advantage. My father has two distinct flaws. He gives Clarissa whatever she wants and is overly concerned with his public image. It is one of the ways Mom got him to agree to a divorce.

"Father, while I'm here, I wanted to talk to you about what I mentioned before. About going to stay with Mom to finish high school? After the wedding, of course." I pause, pretending to think. "I know you'll be busy with your honeymoon and setting up the new house. I wouldn't want to be in the way." I make my tone contrite and conciliatory, trying to sell that I want to be less in the way and not that I just desperately want out of this hellhole.

I can see the glee Clarissa tries to suppress as she approaches my father, her sky-high heels clicking on the wood floor.

"Donny, it's perfect! It really is the perfect solution!"

"What is the perfect solution?" I hear Nathan enter the office. He doesn't even look up as he strides into the room, focusing entirely on the documents before him.

"Jillian is finishing high school at her mother's house. That way, Donny and I can concentrate on the honeymoon and the new house and, oh! Oh!" She actually jumps in place, making me snort. "You two can start with your reelection strategy!" Clarissa ends with a flourish of her hands as if it were all her idea in the first place.

"Lillian," Nathan deadpans.

"Who?" Clarissa's utter confusion makes me roll my eyes.

"Me. My name is Lillian," I say as I raise my hand. Unfortunately, my action draws the attention of everyone in the room. My father sits back down, and I can see him contemplating the decision I just forced upon him. If he says no, Clarissa will throw a fit, Nathan will ask questions, and I know I can cry on command if given the chance. The seconds tick by, and we engage in a stare down. Either way, one of us will be a winner at the end of this, and I plan on it being me. I watch as he looks at the other people in the room before sitting forward.

"Well. It seems like this might be mutually beneficial to everyone. Nathan, should we expect any backlash from it?" While my father may be smiling, I call it his Bruce smile, the giant shark in *Finding Nemo*. That smile never means well for me.

"While news of the divorce had mixed reactions, the photo opportunity showcasing a solid and amicable co-parenting situation can only help."

Humming, he continues to study me. I work to keep my expression blank and bored. If I seem too eager, it will give me away.

"It has been decided that Lillian will complete her high school education with her mother. Havenbrook Academy has a reputation for producing exceptional entrepreneurs. Hence, Nathan, please work with my secretary, Dorothy, to make all the necessary arrangements. Lillian, you can only miss a political event if it conflicts with your school schedule. You will attend all photo opportunities and interviews without any exceptions. This is a nonnegotiable arrangement. Once you have graduated from high school, you will attend Wellesley College. After graduation, we will find you a suitable position in the campaign office or any other place I deem appropriate. Lillian Rose, do you agree with these terms?"

"Yes, Father."

"Perfect!" Clarissa exclaims as she beams around the room. She walks around the desk to talk to me, but I leave the office before she can start. I maintain a blank expression as I calmly walk back to my room. Once there, I close the door and can't help but smile. Finally, I did it! Pulling out a suitcase, I start to pack. It is a few weeks before the wedding, but I will be ready. I have the next three years to live the life I want and figure out how to leave behind the one I don't.

Chapter Three

Jensen

The bonfire is going strong at the McWilliams farm. It is the perfect night to have a party. Dad shocked me when he told me he was getting married, and then he hit me with a double whammy: not only would she be moving in, but her daughter would be as well. For as long as I can remember, it has just been my dad and me. Even when my mother was alive, she only came in and out as work and her many lovers allowed.

To say I was pissed over the upcoming change is an understatement.

Abuela thinks I resent my dad trying to move on. It isn't that. Since moving to Havenbrook, Dad and I have finally started building a real life together. We have a routine, and I have friends, real ones. I am in a band, and we are going to be big. Delilah is the biggest reason things are going as well as they are. I am not ready to change the life we had just begun to build for ourselves with the arrival of someone new.

Looking around, I see Delilah on the other side of the fire, dancing with other girls from our class, her red hair glowing like a second flame in the night. Boys from school hover in her vicinity, just trying to get her attention. They will fail. Her brother's best friend, Alexander, is the only boy who made it onto her radar. Anyone who spends time in the Callahan house can see it, except Alexander. That doesn't stop the idiots from trying. I'm not saying I didn't think about it for about thirty seconds. Something about Delilah draws you in and makes you want to be wherever she is. She's larger than life; it just almost shines around her. However, I'm not stupid. Alexander is the only one for Delilah.

Grabbing my guitar, I get a refill by the keg before settling in front of the fire. I start tuning my guitar, mainly just thinking of something to play. I strum nonsense while staring at the flames, waiting for inspiration. Random notes slowly morph into the new popular '90s rap mashup that has been playing on the radio. Strumming with more purpose, I begin to play the intro again. Several classmates gather around, singing along while the girls get up and dance.

I see her just as I start the chorus. She's new to town, I don't recognize her, and she is visibly nervous. She's approaching the bonfire like she's never seen one. Her long, pale blonde hair falls in waves and curls down her back, glowing like gold in the firelight, and it frames a face that would make angels weep. She's about the prettiest girl I have ever seen, and Savannah high society is not short on cute girls. Big blue eyes dart around, looking at everything and nothing at the same time. She's tiny. If she's five six, she's wearing heels. Some meathead from the football team makes a beeline to her, trying to offer her a drink. She waves him off, stepping back like she's frightened, and it has me tightening my grip on my guitar. I don't like it. At all.

Standing up, I take a step forward.

"Angel."

Both of them look at me, and I cock my head at her, making it clear I want her to come closer to me. Skirting around the fire, she keeps making wary glances at the jock before she reaches me. I grab her hand, shocked that she barely reaches my shoulders, she's shorter than I thought. I move her to the haybale beside me.

Handing her my drink, I lean in and whisper in her ear.

"This is where you sit, Angel. Always with me."

Everyone is paying entirely too much attention to my angel, which makes her visibly uncomfortable, so I decide to fix it. The last thing I want is for her to be anything but comfortable around me. I swing my guitar back around and start up a Wild Child Reckless song known to get the crowds jumping. When Delilah hears the opening notes, she heads over and adds her vocals and the party begins. Everyone is cheering, singing along, and dancing. Everyone except the angel by my side.

Delilah grabs her guitar and transitions us into a set we have been working on. Grayson, our drummer, walks over and grabs an empty keg to make an impromptu drum set, and the party kicks up. Turning to look at the tiny blonde next to me, I motion toward the dance floor. When she shakes her head no,

I return my attention to Delilah, holding up two fingers, our code for tapping out. Delilah gives me a funny look but nods in acceptance. When the song finishes, I stand up, stretching out the kinks in my back before holding out a hand to help my angel to her feet. Her hand is smooth and soft against mine. I walk away from the fire until the noise of the party is replaced by the sounds of the country at night. I can hear the cicadas calling, followed by frogs, crickets, and other critters. I head us toward a tree that fell last winter.

"So, I've never seen you before. Are you new in town?" I prop my guitar up against the tree's stump and turn to face her.

"Don't you think that's a little cheesy as a pickup line?" She trails a finger along the tree trunk, tracking the bark.

"Angel baby, I don't need a pickup line for you. I knew from the moment I saw you that we were meant to be." I watch her like a hawk as she tries to avoid looking at me.

"Hmmm..." she hums. "Yes. I am new to town, that is." My lips quirk at her need to clarify.

"I knew I hadn't seen you before. I would never forget meeting an angel."

"I bet you say that to all the girls."

"Never." My smile drops. I don't want her to think this is even remotely a joke for me.

"Do girls throw themselves at me? Yes. I'm fairly popular and in a band. That combination is basically catnip for high school girls. Have I wanted to have a thing to do with any of them? No.

I wasn't interested in anyone until I met you, angel baby. One look at you, and I knew."

I can see her smile in the dark, and I smile back.

"So, now tell me, angel baby, how did you end up here if you are new in town?"

"Oh. My mother heard about this party and suggested I come out here and try to break the ice with some of my new class-mates. The school I attended last year was a private all-girls academy, and my mom thought meeting some kids this way would make the school year easier." She picks a piece of tall grass out of the ground and twirls it around.

"That's not a bad idea. This is usually where most kids end up on the weekends and over the summer." I walk up and slide both hands around her waist, lifting her to sit on the fallen tree.

"The people who own this place don't mind?" I shake my head, stepping in between her knees; the skirt of her cotton dress rides up, giving me a glimpse of her long legs.

"We clean up after ourselves and keep the noise to a minimum. Kids have been drinking and partying in these pastures for years. It is almost a Havenbrook tradition. I bet the owners partied here when they were our age too. It's a good town and a good school. You'll like it. Promise. I'll introduce you to Delilah. She's the best."

"Delilah?"

"Yeah, she's the redhead I was singing with earlier. She's kind of a local celebrity. Our band is Wild Child Reckless, and we perform all over. This past summer, we had several big gigs. Grayson is our drummer." I tuck her hair behind her ear, sliding my fingers through the curls.

"That sounds exciting. I've never done anything like that before." I cup her warm cheek in mine.

"Stick with me, angel baby, and I will show you a new world of things you have never done before." I slowly lower my lips toward hers, allowing her time to rebuff my advances, but her head lifts ever so slightly. She is as drawn to me as I am to her. I brush my lips gently across hers, barely touching but close enough to feel her gasp against me.

"Jensen, we need you! Delilah is wasted and trying to drive home, and we can't get her to give up her keys!" I curse as Jackson West runs up to us, ruining the moment.

I groan in frustration. "I'm on my way!" Turning back to my angel and run my fingers through her hair one last time. The last thing I want to do is leave her, but I know if I don't, Delilah will end up behind the wheel. Resentment churns in my stomach. I just want to be where my angel is, and Delilah has to go and pull this crap. "I'm sorry, angel baby, but I've got to go. Meet me at the front steps of the school tomorrow morning." Gazing into her bright blue eyes one last time, I turn and grab my guitar, stalking back toward the blaze and rowdy bodies.

I'm almost back to the fire when she says my name on the breeze.

Chapter Four

Lily

"Jensen," I say softly as I watch him stride back to the fire and Delilah. I bring up my thumbnail and chew on it. It can't be a coincidence that the one guy I met at this party is my stepbrother. He didn't recognize me, but why would he? I also never told him my name. Mom and Michael said I would find Jensen here, but I didn't expect this. I can see him in the firelight as he passes his guitar to someone before swinging Delilah in his arms. Her red hair falls in a riot of curls as she laughs gleefully, one arm wrapped around his neck as he holds her secure against his body. Watching them together, something twists in my stomach. They look amazing together.

I step carefully away from our secluded spot and head back toward my vehicle. I return to my car just in time to see Jensen trying to load Delilah into his truck while a blond guy loads their instruments. I sit and watch them in the dark, my breath held. I can hear the murmur of voices, and she seems to be arguing with him. Jensen plops Delilah on the hood of his truck, clearly frustrated. I can't determine what he says to her, but if the hand gestures are any indication, he's chewing her out. Delilah hangs her head. His posture instantly changes, and he pulls her into his arms. That feeling is back, and I bite my nail hard enough that I'm worried I'll break it. I'm jealous. I can't explain it, but I am not sure I want to. When Jensen backs away, I see Delilah swiping at her face. She's crying. Jensen picks her up, and she lets him sit her in the truck's cab this time. Jensen stops and looks toward the fire, and I scoot further down in my seat, pulling my sweater up to my eyes like an idiot. He kicks the ground before getting in his truck, and I wonder if it's because he doesn't see me.

I watch as his red truck pulls away. I sit there thinking over the night before cranking my car and heading home. I pull into the driveway, and the house is dark. I knew it would be; Mom and Michael are out of town. I unlock the door and walk into the silent house. I never knew silence could sound different. Silence used to be cold and unwelcoming, almost surgical. This silence is warm and welcoming, like every good thing that can happen is just asleep, waiting for you to wake it up. I stand in the dark and listen, looking out over the living room. The furniture is not new, it's used and loved. This isn't a house; it's a home. I am trying to remember the last time I had a home, and the thought lingers, heavy in the air.

I walk down the hallway, my hand trailing down the wall. Pictures of a little boy with dark hair and gray eyes, smiling as he plays with a younger Michael, fill the wall. Then he's slightly older and in the kitchen, cooking with Michael, playing guitar, and playing with a dog. All down the hall are pictures of Jensen in different stages of his life, all proudly showcased by his dad. I reach the end of the photos and frown, starting over and paying more attention. When I reach the end again, I am sure there isn't a single photo of Jensen and his mom. I know it has been a few years, but I expect, given the photographic representation of his life, to see at least one photo of him and her. Then again, when my mom left, my father purged every molecule of her from the house.

Pushing the thought to the back of my mind, I open the door to my room and stand in the doorway, examining it. I wasn't allowed to take anything from my room in Austin; it had all been professionally staged along with the rest of the house. Instead, Dad arranged to have a local designer source everything for my room here. Modern furniture gleams in the moonlight, white and clinical. Every item screams money and affluence. This room is so out of place with the rest of the house that it only reinforces how I feel.

"One of these does not belong...." I whisper into the silence.

I open the closet of designer clothes, all with tags still attached, and sigh. I pull out a set of pajamas before heading to the shower. I put my clothes on the counter, shutting the door to my room. Turning, I notice a door on the other side of the bathroom. Curious, I walk over to it and into Jensen's bedroom. The bathroom is a Jack and Jill. I chew on my thumbnail for half a second before venturing into his space.

The room smells like cologne and something earthy. I take a deep breath in and hold it. I tiptoe further, heading to his desk, which is covered with sheet music, guitar pics, and various stationery. Picking up a guitar pic, I wander around the rest of his room. The wall above his desk is a collage of photos, mostly of him and Delilah. They are performing in almost all of them, but there are several candid shots of the two of them. I run my finger over several, lingering on his smile. I pick up random items as I wander around his room. Unlike my room, his room is a hodgepodge of different furniture types and styles; clothes and boots litter the floor and bed, and cowboy hats hang on the wall next to a lone necktie. A noise outside makes me jump, and I rush back into the bathroom, locking the door behind me. I hold my breath and listen. I can't hear anyone moving through the house, but the pounding of my heart makes it difficult to hear anything else. I stay there against the door for what feels like hours, but in reality, I'm sure it is only a few minutes. When I don't hear anything else, I shower for the night.

Climbing into bed, I lay there and stare at the ceiling, torn between conflicting emotions. School starts tomorrow. Mom suggested I try to find Jensen, thinking he would be my guardian angel as I navigate this new school. Now, I just want to avoid him. Even thinking of him makes my skin itch. What is he going to say when he realizes who I am? I'm not naive enough to believe I can avoid him, even in a school this size. Rolling over, I stare out the window and into the dark, my internal conflict mirroring the outside world. Lillian Grace DuPont, what have you gotten yourself into?

Chapter Five

Jensen

After spending the night at Delilah's house, babysitting her drunk ass all night, and then getting up early to grab a change of clothes at my house before picking up Grayson and going back to get Delilah for school, it's a tremendous effort to drag my tired and hungover ass up the stairs. Man I wish I could have been in my own bed.

Looking around for my angel from the party last night, I notice people staring and whispering. Confused, I stop and look around, finally seeing a group of girls giggling in front of one of the Summer Splash Carnival posters—a poster that currently has a larger-than-life picture of me, dripping sweat, from one of our performances over the summer. I halt in my tracks, my jaw on the ground as I read that I will be the featured guest of the dunk tank this year. I hear a giggle behind me, and I whirl around to find Delilah trying hard not to crack up.

I glare at her. "Did you do this, Callahan?"

The cheeky heifer has the nerve to laugh and nod. I stalk up to Dee, fully prepared to give her a piece of my mind, when she flings herself at me. I catch her out of reflex, but she is a freaking spider monkey, and before I know it, her arm is wrapped around my neck and she is dragging me to the ground.

"Whatcha gonna do about it, Parker?" She grunts, trying to keep me on the ground, but I'm many inches taller and many pounds heavier; she doesn't stand a chance. "Hmmm. Nothing, you're going to sit in that dunk tank like a good little bassist, and you're going to like it."

"Delilah Rose Callahan! Jensen Allen Parker!" Principal Tudyk comes flying down the stairs. When we continue wrestling, he pulls a foghorn from his pocket and blows three sharp blasts. "Stop this at ONCE!"

We break apart, panting and laughing hysterically on the ground. Grayson shakes his head at us before heading up the stairs to the front door. I lie here for a few more seconds, my breath sawing in and out of my lungs and a massive smile on my face. Standing up, I dust off my jeans and tuck my shirt back into the waistband. I'm looking around for my backpack when Principal Tudyk clears his throat. Delilah turns with a grin and a tone so sweet, chocolate wouldn't melt in her mouth.

"Good morning, Principal Tudyk. How was your summer?"

I finally spot my bag lying on the ground by the shrubs. Grabbing it, I bolt for the door, taking advantage of Principal Tudyk being distracted by Delilah. Stopping by the main office, I pick up both our schedules. Grayson is there waiting, and we compare really quickly. We all have an A block for the first half before switching, which means we are in the same classes for most of the day—sweet!

I'm hanging around the office waiting for Delilah. What is taking her so long? I head back out to the front, bursting through the double doors.

"Dee, where are you? The final bell has rung, and Mr. Pendle—" I stop abruptly and stare at the sight before me. My angel baby, the girl I was so obsessed with that her every feature haunted my dreams, is standing next to Delilah on the steps.

"Uh, Jensen? Are you okay there, Parker?" Delilah waves her hand before my face, but I don't care. All I can see is my girl, standing there staring back at me, her eyes round and shining. Delilah stares back and forth between us before clearing her throat.

"Jensen, this is Lillian DuPont. She just moved here and will be starting at Havenbrook."

All the blood drains from my head so fast I feel like I might fall. Delilah grabs my arm, but I shake off her hand, spinning abruptly and stalking back into the school, heading straight to my first class.

I'm waiting impatiently for Delilah when second period starts. She sits down and immediately lays into me. "What the hell was that this morning, huh? You looked like you had an aneurysm over the new girl! Do you want me to tell her to get lost or something? Because despite what Tudyk said, I don't have to let her hang out with us."

I jump up so fast at the thought of Delilah kicking Lily out of our group. Before I even register it, I'm in Delilah's face. "You even think about doing anything to her, Delilah, and believe me, girl or not, we will be going rounds." Delilah eyes me warily, grabbing my hand and pulling me back down into my chair. I let her sit me back down but hiss out a warning. "You're my best friend. I love you more than life itself, but this is a line, Delilah Rose Callahan, and I dare you to cross it."

"Okay, seriously, what the ever-loving FUCK!" Delilah throws up her hands in frustration, accidentally shouting across the room. The class goes quiet and stares at us, so I slump down lower in my seat with my elbows on my knees and my head in my hand. "You know I would never do that, right? I'm not that person. I was messing with you to get a reaction. And I definitely got one. So you better start talking. Now." Delilah's tone brooks no argument, and I use the pads of my thumbs to massage my temples.

"You remember how I told you my dad met someone and has been seeing her for a year? And remember how he just sprung it on me that they were dating, but now they are getting married?"

Delilah appears to think back. "Yeah, I remember. You told me the lady was supposed to be coming down over the summer but got delayed and would be here soon. What does that have to do with the price of tea in China, Jensen? Did she show up? Has she been mean to you?"

"No, she's been fine. She showed up last weekend, and I discovered she has a daughter. No one mentioned it before because she lived with her dad. But now she's living here... *with us!*" I can't keep the frustration out of my tone.

Delilah makes a scoffing sound. "Okay, I get how that could be upsetting, but it doesn't explain what happened this morning."

"You remember how we went to the Thompson twins' party at Mathison's place, and I told you about the girl I met?" I have replayed every moment of that night for the past several hours. It was the first time I was glad that Delilah had drug me out to a party.

Dee rolls her eyes. "Yeah, I remember that too. You said she was the most gorgeous girl you ever saw, but she slipped away before you could get her number. What does that have to do with..." Her voice trails off as she realizes where this story is going.

"My new stepsister-to-be is Lillian DuPont, and she's the girl from the party." I hold my head as I confess this, knowing what the alternative is, and that's not an option. Delilah sits ramrod straight in her chair.

"Oh. Fuck."

Chapter Six

Lily

I make it through my morning classes and follow the crowd toward the cafeteria. This school is so different from my private school. Kids laugh and joke in the hall, throwing footballs and wadded-up pieces of paper. The teachers stand around and watch. There is no yelling, no scolding, and, best of all, no uniforms!

I follow the student in front of me and grab a tray off the buffet line. I see there is a salad bar, so I head that way. I have just made myself a salad when I hear a throat clear next to me. "Angel baby, is that all you're going to eat?" I look up into Jensen Parker's heart-stopping gray eyes, and any bit of saliva I had evaporates into dust.

"Oh. Well. Yes. See, Father has me on this special diet and—" Jensen growls at me—legit growls—before dropping a plate with two pieces of pizza and a piece of pie on my tray.

"The last thing you need is to be on a diet. Your father isn't here. Eat." He grabs my elbow and steers me to a table by the window. A few other students give me curious looks, but Jensen glares at them until they give up and return to their conversations. I pick at my salad, staring longingly at the slices of cheese pizza. Jensen watches me pick at my salad until his frustration clearly wins; he steals it off my tray and dumps it into the trash can behind him. "Eat." He picks up his piece of pizza, looking over my shoulder, but drops it when he busts out laughing.

Turning to look behind me, I see a limping Delilah walking into the cafeteria, flipping him off. She grabs a tray before sitting across from me and next to Jensen. I can't help but watch her. She's larger than life, always moving, talking, and just ALIVE—basically, everything I am not.

I watch as she elbows Jensen before pointing her fork at him. "Just keep laughing, bass boy. Have you forgotten?" Delilah jumps up on the table and announces to the room, "Ladies, this weekend only, the one you've been waiting for. Mr. Jensen Parker, bassist for Wild Child Reckless, will be the feature star of the Summer Splash dunk tank! Save up your dollars! He won't come cheap!" Girls start cheering, and a few boys, too, but the murderous look on Jensen's face when she sits back down has me hunching in on myself and looking anywhere but at him.

"So, Lillian. You're coming to the Summer Splash Carnival this weekend, right? It's the biggest summer event in Havenbrook. There's so much to do! Rides, food vendors, a silent auction, raffles, plus all the local artisans set up stalls." I blush under her verbal barrage, but Delilah continues on. "I love the magnolia and honey bar from Soaps and Ropes. They're a local dude ranch specializing in making handmade goat milk soaps that smell divine!" I perk up at this. I love handmade soaps. They are so much better on my skin, and I prefer their scents to the fancy designer products Father makes me use. But he's not here now.

I bite my lip, looking down at my hands and sighing. "I don't know. I may have to attend some events with my dad this weekend. I hope I'll be able to go to the carnival instead, though. I was wondering why it is called the Summer Splash Carnival when it happens in September?" I wince, knowing I must endure the tirade if I don't go to the gala with him.

Delilah, however, is a sweetheart about answering. "Well, you see, we have a carnival just about every season—Spring Fling, Fall Festival, Christmas Carnival—and the city wanted to do something for summer but it is just so darn hot. Since the official last day of summer generally falls in September and that just so happens to coincide with Texas turning down the heat, they decided that would be the perfect time!" Delilah shrugs like this should make perfect sense, and I guess for someone who has lived here their whole life it does. "I hope you get to go. I'll text you, and we can ride together if you can come."

I'm sure she is only trying because of my relationship with Jensen, but I appreciate the gesture nonetheless. It's more than anyone else has ever done in my life. Jensen slams his drink down before standing abruptly, throwing his tray away, and stalking outside. My eyes widen in shock, and I look at Delilah for guidance, but she shrugs and returns to her lunch.

I was able to get out of the gala citing schoolwork due to the transfer. Although I am actually ahead. Turns out Havenbrook is behind my previous prep school and I was actually able to use the past week to get acquainted with the town I find myself in. I park my car, watch the people streaming into the square, and feel the color draining from my cheeks. I HATE crowds. Why did I think I could do this? Mom even encouraged me, giving me cash to get something I wanted. I didn't have the heart to tell her father sent me with a platinum credit card. Not because he wanted to ensure I was taken care of; it's all for appearances. I see Jensen setting up on the stage, so I wander over, but not too close. He acts like he doesn't see me, but I can feel his eyes when he thinks I'm not looking. I spot the stall Delilah was talking about, Soaps and Ropes, and I edge closer to glance at their offerings.

"This is the one you want." I jump, squealing at the voice behind me. I turn quickly and bump right into Jensen's broad chest. He's holding a soap bar for me, and I look at the label Whispers of Spring—a mixture of fresh goat milk, lily of the valley, freesia, and oatmeal.

"This sounds lovely. Thank you." I reach for my purse to pay for the soap, but Jensen beats me to it, handing the lady a bill before taking my elbow and moving me stageside.

"You sit here." He points to a chair before he leaps back up on the stage, his forearms flexing with the movement. Looking around, I can see I am not the only one who noticed and feel a little anger. This surprises me since it has always been drilled into my head that good girls don't get mad. It's bad manners.

Jensen picks up his guitar and tunes it while Delilah walks up to the mic. "Hello, Havenbrook! How do you love the carnival so far?" People shout in response, so she grins and continues. "I already got the first funnel cake of the season, so you missed out! Don't worry, Maisie will make her delicious treats all weekend!" Delilah knows how to work a crowd, and being the daughter of a politician, I can spot the talent at 200 yards with both eyes closed. Delilah swallows roughly, looking nervous. I glance around, looking at what could have thrown her, only to see a dark-haired man standing on the opposite side of the stage from me. He is staring at Delilah with an intensity that I have never seen before and have only heard about in the romance novels the girls at school whispered about I don't know who he is, but he's thrown Delilah for a loop.

They play for three hours straight, and I admit, they're good. They're going places. Everyone is drenched in sweat but smiling as Delilah reminds the crowd about Jensen being part of the dunk tank. He gives a short wave before jumping down and walking over to me, ignoring all the girls clamoring to get his attention. "Did you enjoy the show, angel baby?"

I can't help but blush. He's so intense. "Jensen, you ignored all those people trying to get your attention."

He glances over his shoulder at the crowd and shrugs, returning to me. "They're not important. I asked you a question, angel baby. Did you enjoy the show?"

How can I possibly tell him how much I enjoyed his show? I don't have the words to describe what it was like to see him perform in person, especially to a crowd this size. "It was magical. I have never seen anything like it before in my life." Jensen hands me a water bottle before pulling me up from the chair.

"Well, I am sure it can't compare to some of the concerts you've seen before, but we are very popular in the area. We've actually had a few labels reach out about signing with them, but our parents are insisting we wait until graduation."

"I've never been to a concert before." Jensen stops suddenly, and I run into his arm.

"What do you mean you've never been to a concert before?"

I grab my bag and scuff the ground with my toes, shrugging. "I mean, I've been to the opera, ballet, and campaign fundraisers, but I've never been to a concert like this. This was my first time."

At this news, Jensen can't seem to stop his grin. "Are you saying I'm your first, angel baby?" I blush bright red and stutter over my words. Thankfully, Jensen takes pity on me, tucking my hair behind my ear. "I'm just teasin', baby. That's all." Someone calls his name, and he looks up before rolling his eyes.

"Look. I've got to do this. Can you hold my phone and stuff, and I'll get it back from you afterward?" I nod and take the items, watching him stalk toward the dunk tank. The line wraps around the square. I can see Jensen glaring at a laughing Delilah. It takes several tries, but when someone finally hits the mark and dunks him, he erupts from the tank, spraying Delilah and the dark-haired man from earlier. They're laughing as they try to wring the water out of their clothes, so Jensen cups a double handful of water and drenches them again. Delilah tries to run but slips. I cry out, too far away to help, and Jensen tries to dive out of the tank, but the man catches her, pulling her close. They stand there, almost like they're in a trance, for several minutes before stepping apart. Jensen climbs back on the seat while Delilah and the mystery man walk away. Feeling eyes on me, I look up, and Jensen is staring at me. I give a small wave before pretending to look at the vendor behind me. Coming here may have been a bad idea.

Chapter Seven

Jensen

I am stuck in that dunk tank for over two hours. Lucky for me, at this time of year in Texas, it is still blazing hot, so the tank's cold water feels refreshing. Lily looks bored as she browses the booths around the dunk tank. She doesn't buy much, just a few more trinkets, so when my time is up and I have changed into the dry clothes I brought, I walk out to find her. I push through the mob of girls trying to get my attention; they mean nothing. I look around but don't see Lily, and I panic. I check the remaining aisles and finally find her standing in front of a painting at a local artist's booth. She's staring at it, clearly lost in thought, and I walk up behind her to view it too. It's a field with a magnolia tree, set against a backdrop of a Texas sunset sky with blues and purples and oranges, and a scattering of clouds. A woman in a white dress is standing under the tree, her back to us, staring out into the distance. Lily reaches out a hand as if to touch the painting before drawing it back, accidentally hitting me in the stomach. "Oh, I am so sorry! I didn't mean to."

"Didn't mean to what, angel baby? Assault me? Please do so any time you want. I love the feel of your hands on me. You never have to apologize for touching me." I nod at the painting. "You going to buy it? It's beautiful. I think I know where it was painted. There is a tree like that on the Winchester Mansion. They used to do weddings there all the time, but then Old Man Winchester died. His kids live in some big city and have no interest in the property. They tried to sell it a few times, but it always fell through. You wanna go there? No one will mind."

Lily blushes. "Father wouldn't approve of the painting; he says art is an investment, and the only time you should buy art is when it will be worth something someday."

I can't help but snort. That is the dumbest reason I have ever heard to buy a painting. "Baby, you buy art because it speaks to you. Because you lose yourself in it and never want to find yourself again. You buy art because you love it. It doesn't matter if no one else does because you do. You buy art for YOU." I hold her by the shoulders, massaging them as she stares at the painting, gnawing on her lower lip in indecision. I pull her lip down. "Lily, do you want the painting?" She gives it one more longing look but shakes her head, and I sigh. "Okay, well, let's get you back to your car so you can head home. I have to do a few more things with the gear, but you're getting pink. I don't like it. Where is your sunscreen?" I steer her away, but not before getting the attention of the artist and pointing at the painting and then to myself. I scold her lightly to keep her distracted as I walk her back to her ridiculous little car. The fact that she even has a car this small in a town like Havenbrook screams that she isn't local, but it does suit her.

Once I have her back in her car and headed home, I swing back by the tent to purchase the painting. The artist—an old man who has been painting art for this town since my dad was a boy—smiles at me. "That's a sweet girl you have there, Jensen. She came up timid and polite and wanted to know if she could look around. like I was going to tell her no. She saw that there painting, and she was gone. She stood there and stared at it for, I don't know, it must been near twenty minutes. I'm glad you're buying it for her. It doesn't seem right for anyone else to own it."

"Thank you, Mr. McCrae. I appreciate you holding it for me until I got back. It is the Winchester place, isn't it?" I put my wallet back in my pocket and pick up the package.

"Yeah, it's Winchester's place. You were right about that. It's a shame that house going the way it is. It was a thing of beauty back in my day; see here?" He flips through a stack of paintings, pulling out one of a stately home. Large windows are framed with blue shutters, and a small balcony comes off the master suite. The windows are open, a small breakfast is laid on a side table, and the curtains look like they're blowing in an imaginary wind.

"Oh wow, this is what it used to look like?" It's gorgeous. Nothing like the moss- and algae-covered building it is today.

He nods sadly. "Yup, it was the spot growing up. Mrs. Winchester was so proud of it; there was a flower garden in the back, and it was the talk of the town. It got featured in many magazines too. It is a shame." Someone else walks up, so he steps away, and I wave goodbye.

I finish with the rest of our gear, carefully tucking the painting into my truck. I swing by Abuela's house to pick up tamales and head home. Opening the door, I am greeted by silence and a note on the side table saying that Dad and Gwen went to dinner in Riverbend. Sighing, I head down the hallway only to pull up short at the sound of the shower running. There is only one person it could be. It takes every ounce of self-control I've perfected over the last sixteen years not to barge into that bathroom and do something I definitely will NOT regret but should NOT do. Instead, I place the painting against her pillows before closing her door quietly. I head into my bedroom and try to concentrate on my math homework. I open my book and then catch a whiff of her soap. It is the one I bought her, and I can't help the groan that escapes my mouth.

I can't stay here alone with her, I'm not a saint, so I grab what I need and head over to Dee's house. I can crash there for the night, far away from golden-haired angel that smells like lilies and forever. I grab a piece of paper and jot a quick note down just in case anyone comes looking for me. I've spent countless nights at Dee's house, so I know Dad won't care. They probably won't be home until late anyway. Dad never visits Riverbend without stopping at the Lone Star Sweets bakery. The owner is a single mom, and Dad always said she was the hardest-working woman he had ever met. I thought she was the best baker I have ever met, although I would never admit it to my abuela.

I have just grabbed my jacket when I hear the shower shut off. I curse quietly when I realize my guitar is still in my room. There is no way on God's green earth that I am going back into that room. I snatch my satchel off the hook and stomp outside, locking the door quietly behind me. I will just have to come and get it tomorrow. I don't think we're meant to practice, but you never know when Dee will get a bee in her bonnet and want to. However, she is supposed to be shopping with Alexander tomorrow, which may keep her sufficiently occupied and out of my hair.

Chapter Eight

Lily

I am in the middle of my shower when I think I hear something. I freeze for a minute, straining to listen over the running water, but I continue with my bath when I don't hear anything else. The soap that Jensen picked out earlier is decadent.
The light floral scent is lush without being overwhelming, and
the added oatmeal helps exfoliate my skin until the only pink
left is from the hot water.

Shampooing my hair is always an ordeal, and I once again long
for the ability to cut my hair into a much more manageable style,
though I know Father would never approve. When I get done
rinsing, I step out, wrapping one towel around my body and
another around my hair. I should blow dry it tonight to avoid
suffering the hair straightener tomorrow, but I don't have it in
me after today. I slip into my pajamas and slippers before exiting
back into my room. I pull up short noticing the painting on
my bed. That was not there when I got in the shower! It's the
painting from the carnival—the one Jensen tried to convince
me to buy for myself. When I saw it, it was the most beautiful

painting I had ever seen. I can't explain it, but it felt like I had seen and lived it before.

I walk up to my bed and caress the painting carefully. The brush strokes are rough against my fingertips. Jensen bought it for me; that much is obvious. Which means he was here in my room. Turning, I look at his door on the opposite end of the bathroom and bite my lip again. I walk up to the door and knock, waiting for an answer. When no one calls out, I knock a bit louder, only to be met with more silence. I crack open the door. "Jensen? Are you there? I wanted to say thank you for my painting." When I don't receive an answer, I poke my head in to see an empty bedroom. I stand there in confusion for a moment. He had to have been home; he brought the painting.

I walk into the kitchen, but it is empty, and there is a note on the bar. I pick up the paper, scanning the contents, and my heart hits my feet. Jensen is spending the night at Delilah's. I may be naive, but even I know the guy you like spending the night at another girl's house is not a good sign. I drop the paper and head back to my room. I transfer the painting to my desk and curl up in bed, staring at it. The more I stare at the painting, the more I can swear I see the light moving across the field. Fanciful, entirely fanciful. When I can feel my eyelids getting heavy, I sigh, burrowing deeper under my duvet. Tomorrow, I will put my foot down; tomorrow, I will tell Jensen to leave me alone.

When I wake up the following day, it smells of something unique and eggs. I pull on my robe and stumble into the kitchen to see my Mom and Michael dancing around the room to the radio. Michael pulls her close and kisses her softly; Mom only pulls back when she realizes I am standing there. She's blushing, which I find incredibly adorable. "Don't let me bother you; I just need to get me a coffee." I grab the carafe and return to the bar. I pour a mug, adding a generous helping of vanilla creamer. I take a deep sip and sigh as I can feel my neurons start to fire.

"A fellow coffee drinker! Welcome! Again, I just want to say I am *so* glad you're staying with us, and if you need *anything*, please let me know!" Michael comes around and hugs me tight, and I can feel the tears clogging the back of my throat. Besides my mom, my nanny was the last person who hugged me, and that was when I was four. I clear my throat before forcing a smile. "Thank you for having me, really. I promise to stay out of the way and not cause too many issues."

Mom walks around the bar. "Oh, baby, no. Don't think like that! I am so happy you got your father to let you spend this time with us! I have missed you." She pulls me close, and I close my eyes, breathing in her unique scent. I have always loved it, and when she left, I hid the few articles of clothing I found and would sometimes hug them at night when the loneliness was too much.

I sip on my coffee, and Michael sets a plate down in front of me, but besides the eggs, I have no idea what it is. "Oh, thank you, but I normally don't eat breakfast." I grab the fork and turn the eggs around. "I'm not sure what it is exactly... it looks delicious... but really I—"

Michael chuckles. "It's migas. Your mom insists on them most mornings. Just try a bite and let me know what you think. Promise you won't hurt my feelings if you don't like them." He crosses his heart and winks at me before returning to the dishes. I fork up a pile of fluffy eggs and try a bite, but I have to close my eyes as I moan. I quickly cover my mouth as both Michael and Mom laugh.

"Well, Michael, I think we found someone who appreciates your cooking as much as I do."

"These are amazing! OMG!" I fork up another bite, and before I know it, the plate is empty. I blink, looking at the empty dish in shock. I can't remember the last time I ate breakfast. My diet just didn't have room for the calories.

Michael dishes me another serving and winks. "Eat up. Today is the last day of the carnival. You may wanna meet Jensen there." I move the eggs around on my plate, pretending to be casual, which is about as far from the way I feel as possible.

"So, Jensen isn't here? I didn't hear him come home last night."

Michael shakes his head. "There was a note. He spent the night at Delilah's. I don't know why I even keep a room for him here. He's always over there."

The eggs turn to sawdust on my tongue at the fact of Jensen's penchant for sleeping at Delilah's house. I take a sip of my cold coffee before getting up from the bar. "I think I am going to get dressed at head out. Thank you for breakfast." I force myself to smile until my bedroom door closes.

Chapter Nine

Jensen

I was waiting in the parking lot for Lily to pull up at the carnival. She has been trying to avoid me , but I won't let her. I know she thinks having a relationship with me would be wrong, but I disagree. Nothing that feels this inevitable could be wrong. I have made it my mission to wear her down, and I think it's working. We're touring the stalls and I sigh as Lily pulls me to a stop again. Her pert little nose is scrunched up in displeasure, and it takes everything I have not to kiss the look off her face.

"What is the matter, angel baby?"

"I want to look at a pair of earrings over there." Lily tugs again, trying to get me to release her hand, but I refuse to give it up. Before I know it, I will have to be up on that stage, so I will take every second I'm allowed to feel her silken skin against mine. I rub my thumb against the underside of her wrist, feeling her pulse beating like a hummingbird wing.

"Jensen. We have to stop, and we can't do this."

My head snaps up. "Do what, angel baby? Buy you presents? Keep you close to me and safe? Make sure that you are happy and taken care of? That's my job." I crowd close to her and see her pupils expand, leaving only a tiny ring of blue. "You don't want to take my job away, do you, angel baby?" I move my hand up to her jaw, caressing it gently, assisting her in shaking her head no. I find that not giving Lily too much time to think about things is the best course of action. She wants me close but she's still scared of how it will look. "I didn't think so. Now, let's go look at these earrings." I caress her ear, noticing the plain silver hoops.

This seems to snap something in her. "Jensen. No. I don't need more earrings. The last thing I need is for you to buy me earrings. I have dozens of pairs. What I need is for you to listen to me. Please."

Sighing, I stop again, turning to face her. "Okay, angel baby. I am listening. What did you want to tell me?"

Her nose is wrinkled again, and she goes as far as to stamp her tiny foot. "We can't do this Jensen! My mom is marrying your dad! That means you're soon to be my brother! Whatever this is, we can't do it!" She gestures between our bodies, and I have to frown.

"First, I am not your brother; I will never be your brother. You need to understand that right now. I am the man who will take care of you for the rest of your life. The sooner you accept this, the better it will be for both of us. Second, I can and will do what I want when it comes to spoiling you, angel baby. We both know you can buy anything your heart desires. I am under no illusion that you need my money for anything. However, it makes me happy to buy you presents and spoil you, so you'll let me do that, won't you?"

I can hear Delilah tuning her guitar on stage, and I curse out loud. "I have to go. Wait for me in the same place as last time. I will find you after the set." I kiss her on the forehead before striding off through the crowd. The last thing I want to be doing right now is performing. I stride up onto the stage and grab my guitar. Delilah shoots me a look, and I give her a tense smile. I picked her up from shopping with Alexander and she gave me hell about my relationship with Lily. She didn't much appreciate it when I told her she shouldn't throw stones from her glass house. Delilah acted dumb, but we both know that her crush on Alexander is more than that. She just refuses to admit it. She is so fucking stubborn.

Grayson counts off the beat, and we roll into the opening of "Red High Heels" by Kellie Pickler. Delilah thinks it funny because she would rather be caught dead than be in anything other than a pair of boots. We are near the end of the set when I glance to the side of the stage to see that Lily isn't there anymore, and I almost miss the chord progression. I start scanning the crowd for her blonde head, but I don't see her. I growl in the back of my throat and head toward the front of the stage. I stalk back and forth, and that's what I see her. She's at the funnel cake truck, and Chadwick from the football team has her backed up against a picnic table. She's looking around desperately, but no one notices with Delilah on stage. I whip my guitar off, lay it on the stage, and jump off. I shove through the crowd and round on Chadwick with a quick right to the jaw. He's a bruiser, but I catch him on the back foot, and he stumbles away. "Go to Delilah." I grab Lily's arm and push her toward the stage.

"Whatcha doing with my girl, Chadwick?"

Chadwick rears around and sneers at me. "Your girl? She is no one's girl. I was talking to her. It's a free country. I can talk to her if I want." I lunge at him again, tackling him to the ground.

"That's where you're wrong, asshole. That's my girl and talking to her isn't free; it's about to cost you your ass." I swing my fists, punching his face until I'm pulled away. Alexander and Grayson yank me off him while two of his football cronies help him up. He's got a busted nose and a split lip, and my knuckles are scraped and bleeding.

The crowd around us murmurs as we glare across the space at each other. Chadwick shrugs off his buddies, muttering as he walks away. "Whatever, man, she isn't that cute anyway. Ice princess material." I lunge at him again, but the guys hold me back. Lily walks up, places a hand on my chest, and I instantly settle down.

"It's okay, he didn't do anything. He was just talking. I promise." Her bright blue eyes stare up at me, moving over my face, making sure I am not injured. Lifting my hand, she uses a napkin to wipe away the blood. "Oh, your poor hand. How will you play? You shouldn't have done that, Jensen." I let her fuss over me because it calms me down to have her nearby.

Grayson and Alexander back away, but I don't care. All I care about is the blonde angel cleaning up my scraped knuckles while simultaneously chewing me out.

"That is where you are wrong, Lily. I did have to. Anyone who disrespects you disrespects me, and I can't let that stand. You are my girl, and I will kick the ass of every male in Havenbrook to make it known."

"Jensen, seriously. You're talking crazy. You can't go around doing things like that. It just isn't proper." Lily is exasperated, and I think she suspects I might be kidding, but little does she know, I am dead serious and will back up my words.

"I don't think I much care about what is proper when it comes to you, angel baby." Lily rolls her eyes, and I take the opportunity to pull her against my chest. I take a moment to enjoy the feel of her in my arms. Lily blushes when she realizes we are still the object of some intense scrutiny. I reluctantly let her pull away but snag her hand at the last second. "C'mon. Let's go see how mad Delilah is at me." I wink at her to let her know I'm not worried, and Lily obediently follows me to the stage.

Delilah is in rare form and calls me the 'biggest doofus she has ever had the displeasure of knowing' and 'as useful as tits on a boar hog.' She then settles down and asks if I'm okay. Seeing my hand sets her off again. Grayson and Alexander have to herd her away from the stage and into the parking area as her language becomes more colorful. She really must have been a pirate queen in a past life.

Lily looks increasingly dejected, and tears are swimming in her eyes when Delilah is led away. "Is Delilah mad at me too? It's my fault this all happened. I should have stayed by the stage, but I just wanted to get a snack. I didn't mean for all this to happen." My heart stutters as I pull her close to me.

"No, no, angel baby. Delilah is just.." I search for the words but come up empty. "She's just Delilah; you must understand she isn't mad. She's upset and worried, and that is how she lets it all out. She will be right as rain in a few hours, but I can tell you with one hundred percent certainty that she is not the least bit upset with you. You had every right to go get a snack without being accosted by a meathead Neanderthal." I tilt her chin up until she finally meets my eyes. "Tell me you understand." Lily bites her lip and looks down, avoiding my gaze. "Uh, uh, uh. Look at me." When her eyes meet mine again, I smile. "Perfect. Tell me you understand, angel baby."

"I understand," Lily whispers, but I can still see the doubt in her eyes. I tug her closer, and we stand there for a minute.

As much as I enjoy holding her, I can hear her stomach rumble. My girl needs to eat, and she will do it in peace this time. "Come on, angel baby. Let's go get you something to eat. How about a chipped beef sandwich plate? Maybe some peach cobbler for dessert? The truck down at the end does the fried cornbread rolls. They're amazing." By the time I stop talking, we reach the truck in question, and Lily's eyes are the size of saucers.

"There is no way I can eat all of that. My father would kill me." I growl low in my throat. At this rate, her father has a lot of explaining to do, but I don't want to worry Lily about it, so I turn to her, smiling.

"Let's split a plate then; I'll finish whatever you don't want." I place the order, and we sit down, and I divide up the food. Despite Lily's protest, she eats most of the peach cobbler. When I wipe her chin with a napkin, she blushes, but I take the opportunity to stroke the petal-soft skin of her cheek. "Can you come with me? I want to show you something." When she nods, I throw away our trash and lead her to my truck.

Chapter Ten

Lily

I follow Jensen to his truck, and he helps me climb inside. Sometimes, I hate being so short, but it isn't like this was something I could pick. Jensen climbs behind the wheel, cranking the car, and we navigate carefully out of the parking lot. He holds my hand tight over the center console, and I try to pay attention to anything besides the warmth of his skin and the smell of his cologne in the truck. Just about then, the radio switches over, and Jensen begins to sing along with the song.

"Your voice is amazing." It truly is a deep, rumbly baritone that gives me goosebumps. "Why don't you sing any songs with the band?" Shockingly, Jensen's cheeks flush.

"I never craved the limelight," Jensen confesses, his voice a bit hoarse. "I always knew we'd make it big, but Delilah'd lead the way. I love being part of the group, and I love Delilah. She's my best friend, who truly deserves to shine." His humility and selflessness make my heart ache a little.

"You deserve to shine too, Jensen," I tell him, my voice filled with emotion. Hearing him say Delilah is the only one who deserves to shine is bittersweet. The truck's movement catches my attention, and I realize we're driving through a field. "Where are we going?" Jensen shoots me a grin before turning back to the road.

"You'll see in just a few minutes, angel baby." He pulls up at the end of the field, where an old wooden gate hangs from its posts. Jensen hops out of the truck and jogs over, opening my door for me before I have a chance. Lifting me down, he holds me close, and I can smell the warm sunshine and a hint of cologne from his shirt. Taking my hand, he leads me to the gate, jumping over before lifting me. Part of me wants to be annoyed with how easily he moves me where he wants to, but the other part likes feeling small and delicate compared to him.

Reclaiming my hand, he leads the way, striding confidently through the overgrown grass. However, I walk more carefully, and my ballet flats are not the best footwear for traipsing through a field. A wry grin slips my lips as I think about all the designer shoes in my closet. I don't actually own anything suitable for walking in a field. Noticing that I am lagging behind, Jensen looks back and frowns. "Why didn't you say you were having issues?" Without another word, he picks me up and carries me the rest of the way up the hill.

As we crest the top, my breath catches at the landscape stretched out before me. Rolling hills, tall trees, stone fences covered in moss, and round hay bales are all brand new to me but strangely familiar, like a dream I can barely remember. I stare at it all in wonder before my eyes catch on a tree just a few paces away and a gasp leaves my throat. It's the magnolia tree, the one from the painting. I turn back to the fields before me in recognition. That's why they looked familiar; this is the real-life version of my painting.

"Jensen...." My voice is choked as he walks up behind me, sliding his arms around my waist, pulling me back against his chest, and I let him. At this moment, in this very second, there is nowhere else I would rather be. For just a moment, just one fleeting incredible moment, I dream that this could be my life. That there is no deal, no balls, no governor's mansion. There is only this boy and this effortlessly simple life. When my phone rings with my father's personal ringtone, I groan. Of course, he would ruin this. Just like he ruins everything good I ever have in my life. I hold a finger up to Jensen and answer the phone a few steps away.

"Hello, Father." I keep my tone cool and calm.

"Lillian, finally. I am a very busy man. I don't have time to wait for you to answer a call all day." His tone is clipped and annoyed. I can't react, though.

"I'm sorry, Father."

"Yes. Yes. Yes. Now, I have a campaign party coming up at the house next weekend. Black tie, obviously. I need you to be here. Some people want to meet you. I have cleared you to leave early from classes to get here in time to meet with hair, makeup, and wardrobe." I can feel my lips turning down in displeasure. I hate campaign parties. Old men stare at me and comment like they think I can't hear. I still remember one time when one of them burst into my room while I was asleep, drunk, possibly more than drunk, and he had to be removed by security. The memory still makes my blood run cold.

"Of course. I will be there." I would rather eat a pickle, but I can't tell him.

"Good. I have to go now." He hangs up without any further interaction, and I sigh as I slip the phone back into my sweater pocket.

"Everything okay?" Jensen walks up, and I find myself leaning into him, seeking his comforting presence. I sigh. How do you explain to someone with a loving father that your father would gladly trade you for a guaranteed win in the electoral races? That he may be trying to do just that scares me, a fear I can't shake off.

"Yeah. It will be. I have to do this thing for my father next weekend. I don't want to, but…" I shrug. "I kinda don't have a choice."

"What do you mean you don't have a choice? You always have a choice!" Jensen's tone is indignant, and I have to smile.

"It was part of the agreement when I got to move in with Mom. I had to promise to attend all campaign events. It's an election year. It isn't that big of a deal. Just a boring party with tiny portions of food and too many people." Jensen is still glowering at the situation, and I force myself to smile, trying to calm him down. "I promise. It's okay. I will be home Sunday, so maybe we can go get something to eat? I saw a diner here in town. Maybe we can go there?"

"Oh. No. Sundays we usually eat at my abuela's house and I already told her we would be there. If I don't show up, she will take a chancla to me. She has an excellent arm, and her aim is scary. However, she makes the best enchiladas you have ever tasted, and her pan de polvo has won awards." I can feel my mouth watering the more he talks.

"I don't think I have ever had enchiladas, and I am not sure what pan de polvo is, but if it is award-winning, it has to be good." We start to wander back toward the gate, but Jensen suddenly stops. I am paying more attention to where my feet are stepping than I realize, and I slam right into his back.

"What do you mean you don't think you've ever had enchiladas?"

Jensen is staring at me, and I can feel my cheeks pinken with a blush. "Well, I mean, that dietitian my father hired didn't like me eating too many carbs, and I had to watch how much dairy I had, so I don't think enchiladas would have been high on her list of approved foods."

"Why on earth would you need a dietitian? You're perfect." Jensen looks at me like I am crazy, and I have to chuckle.

"Because my father is the governor of Texas and has an image to maintain, and that means that I had a dietitian, personal trainer, stylist, and tutor. I attended an all-girls private academy. Most of the girls there didn't want anything to do with me unless their parents wanted to try to get close to my father. It took a lot for me to realize that this was happening, and I was burned more than once when I thought someone was a friend when they weren't. I wasn't allowed to be upset to show that anything was wrong; anything I said or did was potentially gossip fodder. In the end, it was better to keep to myself."

Jensen clenches his jaw but turns, and we return to the truck. Glaring at the ground, he picks me up again and eats up the remaining distance in long strides. "We need to get you proper footwear."

I find myself on the truck side of the gate again, and I can't help but laugh. "Jensen, these shoes cost $400. They're the latest fashion."

Jensen opens my door before lifting me into the truck, barely glancing at my shoes when I point my toes at him. "I said proper footwear, not designer. Something tells me you have more than enough designer clothing to wear. You need some real clothes. Don't worry, angel baby. I'll take care of that." Climbing into the driver's seat, Jensen cranks the truck, and we head back toward town. "You never did get your snack earlier. Let's go get you something to eat, angel baby." Reaching out, he clasps my hand in his, and I can't help but smile as I watch my tree grow smaller in the distance, feeling content in Jensen's company.

Chapter Eleven

Jensen

As we bump along the dirt track heading away from the Winchester house, I grit my teeth to keep my temper in check. I may not have been able to hear everything her so-called father said on that call, but what Lily revealed after lit the fuse on my temper, and I was desperate not to lose it on the sweet angel in the seat next to me. Dietitian! Personal Trainer! Lily was barely 100 pounds soaking wet! She didn't need a dietitian and a trainer. She needed a good barbeque and some cobbler. Or my abuela's tamales and horchata! Something! One thing is for damn sure. I am going to speak to my dad when we got home!

We pull up in the driveway when my phone begins to chirp incessantly. I check the first notification, then clear the rest, pulling it out of the holder and sliding it into a pocket.

"You're not going to answer that?" Lily unclips her belt and picks up her purse. I shrug my shoulder before walking around and opening her door.

"It's just Delilah. I'll answer her later." I help Lily down again before I grab my book bag from the back of the truck. It may be Sunday, but I slacked on schoolwork all weekend, and it will be hell to catch up. I snag her hand again as we walk up the driveway to the house.

"We're home!" I announce as we walk in the front door, tossing my keys into the glass bowl on the entrance table. Lily tries to tug her hand free to skirt around me, but I hold it tighter.

"Jensen," Lily hisses at me, pulling her hand harder. "Someone is going to *see*."

"You think I care, angel baby? Let them see." My casual tone seems to make her mad, and she manages to wrench her hand from mine.

"I care. The last thing I want to do is give my mom a reason to send me back to my father after all it took to get here. The same goes for you touching me and being possessive in public. The last thing I need is a picture of us online and Father's press corps to see it."

Her words pull me up short. "She can't do that." The very thought of someone making Lily leave has my hands clenching.

"If she thinks something is going on that shouldn't be, she will send me back faster than you can blink. I don't want to; getting here cost too much." Lily looks up at me, the beginnings of tears swimming in her eyes.

"Okay, angel baby. I'll tone it down at home, but I refuse to stop touching you completely." Lily nods just as my dad comes around the corner.

"Hey, you two! Did you have fun at the carnival?" Seeing Dad in his typical cargo shorts and chef jacket means he is about to head to the café.

"Oh yes, Mr. Parker, we had a blast. I don't remember the last time I went to something like that!" Lily is back to being bright and bubbly, and I eye her carefully.

"That's great, honey, but please call me Michael. I am about to head into the café; there are snacks in the kitchen—I made dulce de leche cinnamon rolls. Before I forget, we're having dinner at the café, so be there at about six, okay? See you guys later!" Tossing his keys in the air and catching them, Dad whistles on his way out the door.

"Hey, Dad! Wait a second!" I jog to catch up with him as he pauses and turns back to me. "Can we go golfing?" Golfing is our secret code when I need to talk to him and don't want anyone else around. We used it a lot when Mom was alive. Golfing was considered a respectable hobby; we were local club members. So whenever things got bad and I needed to talk, we would go golfing and hash things out over the holes.

"Hey, bud. Yeah, sure! You know it! We can manage to get nine in next weekend. Is that soon enough, or do you want to go sooner?" He's concerned. I can hear it in his tone. Lily is looking between us, a slight furrow marring her brow.

"Nah, next weekend is perfect! I'll make sure we're there for dinner." Dad claps me on the shoulder, giving Lily a small wave. The house is silent as the door closes behind him. "Well, angel baby, let's get a snack and maybe see what's on TV, okay?" Without waiting for an answer, I enter the kitchen, where the warm pan of dulce de leche cinnamon rolls are cooling on the counter. The smell reminds me of weekends with my dad, curled up watching cartoons while we ate them fresh from the oven.

"You look happy." Lily's voice breaks my concentration, and I realize that I have been grinning like a lunatic while sniffing a bunch of cinnamon rolls. I can feel myself blushing.

"Sorry. It's just that Dad always made these on Saturdays, and we would watch Saturday morning cartoons." I can feel Lily staring at me intently, and I fumble with my words under her gaze. "Well, it just was a good memory."

"You're lucky to have a memory like that." Her small hand is cold on my arm, and I take it between both of mine.

"Your hand is so cold. I know what will fix that. A warm cinnamon roll." I plate up one on the paper plate next to the pan, and Lily grabs a fork from the drawer below. "What do you need a fork for?"

Lily pauses uncertainly. "Uh, to eat the cinnamon roll? What else would I need the fork for?"

I laugh until I notice the hurt look on her face. I step over and pull her closer to me. "I'm sorry, angel baby, I didn't mean to laugh. I just never heard of anyone eating a cinnamon roll with a fork, but if you want to use a fork, you use a fork. I would use one too, but these usually only last me two bites before they disappear." Lily rolls her eyes and elbows me in the gut.

I pretend she's knocked the wind out of me, and she laughs. I smile back at her and pile three rolls on my plate before grabbing a glass of milk. Balancing my plate on top of the glass, I head into the living room, flopping into the corner of the L-shaped couch. This couch is my absolute favorite piece of furniture in the living room. It is oversized and squishy and was made for cuddling.

I get comfortable before patting the seat next to me. "C'mere, angel baby. Let's find something to watch." I grab the remote as Lily perches delicately beside me, cutting her snack into bite-size pieces. Smiling, I watch as she takes her first bite, but all the humor is gone when she moans at the taste. I'm suddenly laser-focused on her mouth, and all I want to do is see if she is sweeter than the treat she's enjoying. As if she can feel my gaze, Lily glances up, and her cheeks heat at my intense stare. Her gaze falls back to her lap, and she fidgets nervously with her fork.

Clearing my throat, I go back to scanning the movie offerings. "So what are you in the mood for: comedy, romcom, thriller, horror?"

"Not horror." The answer is so immediate that I have to glance at her; her eyes are wide, and if possible, she looks paler. I grab the blanket off the back of the couch and put it around her shoulders, being careful of the plate in her lap. "Okay, no horror. How about *Tomorrowland*? A little Clooney action?" At her nod, I select the film and then get comfortable again. True to my word, it only takes me a few bites before the cinnamon rolls are gone from my plate, and Lily is only partially through her own.

As the opening credits roll, I tug her closer, placing her plate on the coffee table. Lily leans against me, cuddled under the couch blanket, and in this moment, my world feels complete. I find myself watching how her curls fall when she shifts and how the light plays along the faint freckles on her nose. The tilt of her lips when she finds something funny and how her nose wrinkles when she's not thrilled with the movie's plot. She's fascinating. Enchanting. Everything.

Chapter Twelve

Lily

I am so warm and don't want to wake up, but my bed is shaking. Why is it shaking? I swim up from the most fantastic dream when I realize I am not in bed. I'm asleep on top of Jensen, and he is trying to shake me awake.

"Angel baby. We got to head to the café for dinner. It's 5:30. Come on, sweetheart, wake up. I know you're tired, but you've got to eat something." I jerk upright, grasping my head, which is swimming from the sudden movement. "Whoa, are you okay? Don't move." Jensen is right there, concern on his face.

"I'm okay. I just sat up too quickly. I'm sorry." I'm trying to shove my curls from my face, but they keep falling in waves over my eyes. Frustrated, I grab the mess and tie it in a loose knot behind my head. Jensen is smirking at me when I'm done, and I roll my eyes. "So, we need to get going?" I'm trying to remain neutral, but having Jensen this close to me is scrambling my brain.

"We have a few minutes if you want to do something about that." His finger swirls around my head, and I know I should fix my hair. I head to my room and gasp when I see myself in the mirror. Even tied up, my hair is all over the place, and my clothing is twisted. I comb through my hair, add a band to my head to hold it out of my face, and swap shirts to look more presentable.

Swapping my shoes to cute ankle boots, I head back to the living room. "Ready to go?"

Extending his arm in a sweeping gesture toward the front door, Jensen and I head outside. I walk over to my car but get pulled up short. "No, angel baby, you ride with me. Whenever possible, I will drive you where you need to go." I'm led to Jensen's truck and lifted into the passenger seat. "Do you know what you might want for dinner? I know you haven't been here long, but Dad can make you just about anything you want if you don't see anything on the menu that sounds good."

"I haven't thought about it. I will probably have a chicken salad." I feel my phone vibrate and pull it out to see texts from Father with appointment times with the stylists for the party. I sigh, slipping my phone back into my purse and staring out the side window.

"What's the matter, angel baby?" Jensen grabs my hand back up in his, and I shake my head, not wanting to ruin the moment with more of Father's bullshit.

"It's nothing, just some stuff for this weekend. What's your favorite thing to get at the café?" He shoots me a look, and I suspect it's because he knows what I'm doing, but he allows me to change the conversation anyway.

"I think it depends, but my absolute favorite thing that I normally get is the double bacon ranch burger with chili-cheese steak fries. The fries are double fried, so they're extra crispy and don't get soggy under all the chili and cheese. The whole dish is amazing." I can't stop staring at him in amazement, my eyes traveling down to his flat stomach and back up to his face.

"There is no way you eat that and still maintain those abs," I blurt out before I can stop myself.

"Have you been looking at my abs, angel baby?" Jensen is smirking, and I can't help but blush. "It's okay. Look all you want; they're all for you, after all. But to answer your question, yes, I eat that and maintain these abs. On top of going to the gym, I run most mornings, and lugging all the band equipment is a workout."

"Oh! You run?" I perk up. I love running, especially in the morning when the world is sleepy and quiet, and it is just me, my thoughts, and whatever songs are playing on my Country Mix playlist. "Maybe we could start running together? I haven't due to everything happening, and I miss it."

"Sure. We can go running together. I can take you on my normal path, but I need you to promise you won't go without me. Havenbrook is normally a safe town, but I don't want to take unnecessary risks with your safety, so if I am not running with you, I want you to stick to the blocks around the house, okay?"

"I can do that." We pull up to the café, and I go to open my door, but the noise Jensen makes has me sitting back in my seat and waiting for him to come around. He jogs around the front of the truck and opens the door, holding his hand to help me down. "Good girl. I always open your door." When I walk to the front door, Jensen takes my hand and tugs me around to the side entrance. "We go in this way."

Jensen holds the door open for me, and I am assaulted by the delicious smell of home-cooked food and the noise of a fully staffed kitchen. We walk into a space set up like a family dining room. It is a separate room but still connected to the kitchen, and I can tell that it was built with the thought of family eating here between working shifts.

"Jensen!" A young woman with dark hair tucked into a chef hat comes running up. She looks to be in her twenties and squeals as she wraps her arms around him. He hugs her back with equal enthusiasm, and I can feel myself getting mad, which is shocking since the way I was raised, good girls don't get angry. It isn't polite. However, the more I watch her hug and chatter with Jensen, the more I want to punch her in her gorgeous face.

Jensen turns and catches the look on my face. He smirks at me, letting her go, before pulling me closer. "Arianna, this is Lily. Lily, this is my cousin Arianna." She's training to be a chef and works here during school breaks." I can feel the knot that was forming in my stomach easing. She's his cousin, and now that I look closer, I can see more of a resemblance between the two.

It's in the hair and, oddly enough, noses. Then they both smile, and they have the same lopsided grin. Smiling, I hold my hand out.

"It's nice to meet you. Jensen has spoken very highly of your family's restaurant. I am thrilled to be able to try it." Arianna is grinning when she shakes my hand.

"You're a fancy one, aren't you? That's okay. We'll get you sorted. Now," Arianna claps her hands together, and I watch as she moves toward the table, "since it's your first time here, I'll let you browse the menu. Anything you want, we can make. Just let us know if you feel something isn't on the menu." She continues chattering as she sets out plates and glasses of water on the long wooden table. Someone hollers from the kitchen, and she moves back toward the door. "I must get back in there, but I'll let Uncle Mike know you're here." She's out the door with a chipper wave, and Jensen and I are alone again.

Jensen tugs me close and whispers in my hair. "You were jealous of Arianna, angel baby. But you never have to be jealous of anyone. I don't see anyone but you, and I never will again. I told you the other night you were mine, and I meant it. You and me, angel baby? We're meant to be. Now, keep in mind that most of the people who work here are family. Try not to glare them to death." We both laugh, and I sit in the seat he holds out and pick up the menu. The typical Tex-Mex menu has American options for younger kids, like chicken strips and corn dogs. They also have some traditional Mexican dishes and a range of burgers and sandwiches. Father wouldn't be caught dead eating somewhere like this.

I'm reading and flipping through the pages, musing. "I don't see any salads."

"And you won't. My mother would rather shut the restaurant down than put them on her menu." Looking up, I see Michael standing in the doorway.

"I'm sorry. I wasn't trying to be insulting." I close the menu quickly and set it back on the table. I can feel my cheeks heating. Great! First, I get jealous of Jensen hugging his cousin, and now I'm insulting his grandmother! What else can I do to embarrass myself tonight? I go to pick up my glass of water and knock it over. Groaning, I look up at the ceiling. If there is a God, he should kill me now. Jensen jumps up, grabbing towels from the buffet against the back wall, and Michael grabs the towel off his shoulder to help clean up the mess I created.

"I am so sorry." My blush is full-on red now, and I am desperately trying to pick up ice cubes from the table but keep dropping them.

"It's okay. It's just water, no big deal." Jensen and Michael manage to clean up my mess, and we move to the other end of the table, which is dry. "If you want a salad, Lily, I will make one for you. I merely stated that you won't find them on the menu."

I try to answer him, but I can't get anything past the lump in my throat, and I stare at my hands clasped in my lap as I feel the tears burn in my eyes. Why does this always happen to me? The slightest bit of perceived criticism, and I get overly emotional and things go to shit.

Chapter Thirteen

Jensen

When I return from clearing the towels from the table, I see Lily sitting there about to cry. I glare at my dad, but he shrugs his shoulders, his expression showing he's just as confused by her reaction. I sit beside Lily, put my hand on her shoulder, and she flinches back. I glance up at Dad, and his face is grim.

"An- Lily?" I catch myself. "You okay, babe? It was just a bit of water, no big deal." Lily's hair has fallen forward to obscure her face, but I can hear her whispered apology anyway. "No apology needed. Promise. Now, you said you wanted a salad for dinner?" She nods, and I continue. "Okay, so, a salad, with what on it? Diced chicken?" When she nods again, I reach out and tuck her hair behind an ear to see her face. Her cheeks are blazing red, and tears are in her eyes. "Do you want fried or grilled chicken?" I keep my voice soft and bend to catch her eye. I slide my hand along her thigh to her clenched hands, wedging mine in between them until she releases her death grip on them.

"If possible, I would love grilled chicken." Her voice is still quiet, but at least she's talking now. "And I don't know if you have it, but I would love some Italian dressing."

I tip her face up so that she finally meets my eyes. "We have that. So, grilled chicken salad with Italian dressing?" Lily nods, and I tap her nose, giving her a reassuring smile. Dad looks between us thoughtfully, but I shake my head no, and he nods and heads back into the kitchen to make our food.

"Now, angel baby, we're alone. Why don't you tell me what was going on just now?" Lily tries to duck her head again, but I stop her. "Could you look at me, please? I want to figure out what went wrong earlier."

"I was so embarrassed. First, I commented about the menu and then made a huge mess. I was worried Mike would be mad. Father would have been furious if I had knocked over a glass of water like that at dinner." She is wringing her hands, and I wrap my own around them.

"I'm really starting to not like your father, but I want you to listen. Dad isn't like that. I don't think I have ever seen him mad in my whole life. And he would never take it out on you or me if he had been. Promise. Now, I want you to know something, and I need you to take it to heart. You don't have to walk on eggshells with us. We—specifically, I—want you here, and no matter what, this will always be your home." She smiles at me, and I smile back.

Once she's calmed down, we chat about school, classes, and teachers until I hear a voice ringing through the kitchen.

"Where? Where is *mijito*?!"

I groan. Oh no. "I am so sorry," I manage to tell a wide-eyed Lily just before my abuela bursts into the room.

"Jensen! *Mijito*! There you are! Why did you not come to see me!" Abuela pulls up short when she sees Lily sitting next to me. "Oh! You brought Lilita! Que linda! Look at you! Come here, come here, let me see you." Lily casts me a nervous look before standing and walking up to Abuela, who embraces her like a long-lost daughter before spinning her in a circle. "*¡Oh, eres hermosa pero muy delgada!*" She tuts around Lily for another few minutes before hugging her again. "Don't worry, Lilita. We will get you fattened up." Lily looks over her shoulder at me frantically. "Now, I go check on your dinner!" With that, Abuela leaves the room, and Lily looks like she just got ambushed.

"Sorry, that's Abuela. She can be a bit much sometimes." Lily retakes her seat, and I have to laugh at the look on her face.

"Is she always like that?"

I nod. "Pretty much. She's always run the family, but since Abuelo died, she's been... more. At least, that's what I was told. When we came to town a few years ago, I just met her again for the first time since I was little. She means well."

"What did she say about me? I speak some Spanish, but I couldn't understand it."

I tuck a curl behind her ear. "She said that you were beautiful, and she is right. My angel baby is gorgeous."

"Here we go! One double bacon ranch burger with chili-cheese fries, and one grilled chicken salad with Italian dressing!" Dad sets my plate in front of me and a bowl in front of Lily.

Her eyes pop wide, and I look down. It seems like a typical salad: lettuce, tomato, boiled eggs, cucumber, bacon bits, croutons, dressing on the side. "Everything okay, Lily? Did we put something on there you don't like?" Dad asks, looking concerned, but Lily shakes her head.

"Oh, no. I'm sorry. It's not that; I'm just not used to salads being this big."

Dad chuckles. "Well, things are bigger in this part of Texas. Just eat what you can. If you want, you can take the rest home for tomorrow. Enjoy, you two!"

"Hey, Mr. Parker!" Delilah comes strolling into the room, Grayson behind her, twirling his drumsticks.

"Delilah! Darling! I didn't know you were coming! Let me guess—king ranch chicken? Grayson! It's a pleasure as always—bacon cheeseburger?" Dad quickly switches to Sim-Com—signing and speaking at the same time. When Grayson first joined the band, everyone in our immediate families started taking sign language courses. We wanted Grayson to feel every bit as welcome as Delilah and me. I have never been as proud to be my father's son as I was then.

"I didn't know you guys were going to be here," I say.

Delilah pulls up short, looking between Lily and me. "Oh, I didn't realize it would be an issue if we stopped in. We were driving by, saw your truck parked here, and figured you were eating dinner, so we decided to join you. Do we need to leave?"

While I had wanted to have dinner with just Lily, I wave her into an empty seat. "Sit your ass down. Jesus." Grayson is grinning while getting a couple of glasses of water.

"Dude, did you see the latest video numbers? They have almost as many views as your dunk tank videos." If it is possible to sign in smug Grayson would be doing it.

I glare at Grayson, gritting my teeth. "What dunk tank video?"

"The one I took and posted to our VidReel account. You're going viral!"

I pinch the bridge of my nose, fighting the urge to punch him in the face. "Grayson, there wasn't supposed to be a video of me in the dunk tank. It was bad enough, *someone,*" I glare at Delilah, "volunteered me for it in the first place." Grayson shrugs unapologetically.

"Here we go!" Dad sets down the plates. "Lily, your mom is on the way. Everyone okay? Great! I will be back in a minute. I can't wait to hear about what's new with Wild Child Reckless." Dad whistles as he heads back into the kitchen.

"What does he mean what's new? We don't have anything new." Delilah bites her lip, looking at me sheepishly.

"Delilah Rose Callahan! What. Did. You. Do!" Delilah throws up her hands, and I am about ready to reach across the table and strangle her.

"I didn't *do* anything! I just asked your dad to help me check into a few people who had contacted me." She sounds entirely too innocent. I don't trust her.

"Dee."

"Okay. *Fine.* At first, it was just some people reaching out about gigs. Then I got some inquiries from some talent scouts wanting to know what we had coming up because they wanted to come to check us out. I had your dad help me look into the labels so I can ensure which ones we want to do business with. That's all."

I'm floored. Agents? I thought that was something that only happened to sports players. Are we ready for that? We're not even done with school. My brain is buzzing with questions and potential situations.

"Hello, people! I'm here!" Gwen walks in, and I am struck by how similar she and Lily are. They both have light blonde curls and blue eyes. "Lily-bean!" Gwen kisses Lily on the top of her head, and I glance down to see her just quietly eating her salad, her eyes on her food. I nudge her, and she glances up at me, flicking me a small smile before returning to her food.

"Gwennie!" Dad walks in and places two plates of food on the table before kissing Gwen soundly. We all whoop and cheer, which makes Gwen blush. Dad grins before helping Gwen into her seat and taking his own.

"Okay, Delilah, lay it on me. Which of the labels did you think you wanted to invite?" I see Dad got the meatloaf and mashed potatoes, and I roll my eyes. I know what's coming, and sure enough, he scoops up the mashed potatoes and smears them on top of the meatloaf before taking a big bite.

"Well, Mr. Parker, I have it narrowed down to three. Revelation Records—I've been in touch with their representative, Levi—Harmony Haven Records, and DreamWave Studios. So far, they have all been offering fairly similar deals. I haven't gotten anything in writing yet, but once I do, I want to sit down with everyone and go over them." Everyone agrees, and we go back to our dinner.

I glance back at Lily, who hasn't said anything in all this time. I nudge her elbow. "You okay?" She smiles at me and nods, but I don't believe her.

Chapter Fourteen

Lily

I sit at the table, picking at my salad while the conversation flows around me, and my food sits like a stone in the bottom of my stomach. Agents. Labels. That all points to one thing. Jensen will be leaving. The thought of him leaving hurts, but then again, isn't that what I am doing in three years? How are we any different? At least Jensen is going on to reach his full potential.

On the other hand, I am destined to spend my life being a pawn in my father's schemes, a realization that fills me with sadness. I can feel Jensen staring at me, but I keep my gaze on my dinner. He nudges my elbow. "Are you okay?" I nod and smile, but inside, a piece of me is dying. It doesn't make sense. I just met him; why does the thought of losing him hurt so much?

"Hey, Lily-bean!" Mom comes up, and I give her a relieved smile. "I was thinking we could grab some dessert from the cart?" I nod and follow her, and she pulls me close, tucking me under her arm. "How have things been? I know we haven't gotten to talk very much this week. I'm sorry about that."

I wrap an arm around her waist, hugging her close. "It's okay. Things have been going well. I have to go back for a campaign party this weekend. Dad called earlier."

Mom rolls her eyes. "Becoming governor was the worst thing to ever happen to that man." The dessert cart is fully loaded with different treats, many I don't recognize, but I see a bowl of berries with whipped cream on top, and I know that's what I want to grab. I snag it, and Mom points to another dish.

"Grab that one; it's tres leches cake, Jensen's favorite." She grabs two pieces of a dark chocolate cake for her and Michael. When I return to my seat, I set the tres leches cake in front of Jensen, and he rewards me with a large smile.

He leans down to whisper in my ear, "Thank you, angel baby. It's my favorite. Besides you." The warm puffs of air against my skin make me shiver; goosebumps erupt down my arms. Jensen smirks before taking a forkful of cake and getting caught up in a conversation with Grayson.

I watch in fascination as they sign back and forth, only following half of the conversation since Jensen speaks as he signs. Turning to me, Grayson signs something, and I can feel myself blushing. "I'm sorry. I don't know any sign language yet." I shrug, but Grayson smiles and signs again, and Jensen translates.

"That's okay. I can read your lips for now. I was asking how you were liking school so far."

"It's been going good, thanks. That's one of the signs I know." We both laugh as I sign a very rough thank you to Grayson. Slowly, I get included in the conversation, and by the end of the night, my cheeks hurt from smiling so much.

When we leave, the ride home is quiet, with Jensen holding my hand tight in his. Dropping a kiss on my head, he tells me to shower first. He's got to feed the dogs and check on the chickens before bed.

I shower quickly before sitting at my desk to prepare my bag for school the following week. I hear the door shut, the shower start, and I sit there staring at the closed bathroom door like a fool. I quickly braid my hair, turn out the lights, and lay down to sleep. I just lie there in the dark, the only sound being the shower, and I can feel my heart racing. I press my hands to my cheeks and feel the heat radiating. A knock on the door has me jumping. Jensen opens it and sticks his head in, glancing around before coming over to drop down on the side of the bed.

"Good night, angel baby. I'll take you to school in the morning, okay?" I nod mutely, and he leans down, brushing a kiss against my forehead, tucking a loose curl behind my ear. "Sweet dreams." Jensen heads back to his room, closing the door behind him, and I roll over, trying to get comfortable but failing. Frustrated, I flop onto my back, and my gaze snags on my painting that Jensen hung opposite my bed. I stare at it, thinking about the day, until my eyes finally drift closed, and I am lost in the dream that my future is mine to choose.

The week flies by at school, and I wake up Friday morning with a pit of dread in my stomach. I wouldn't say I have ever liked campaign parties, but having been away from the oppressiveness that is my father for the past couple of weeks, I find myself resenting them even more. By lunchtime, I have worked myself into a foul mood. I don't want to leave after lunch and make the long drive back to the mansion. I slam my tray down a little more forcefully than intended on the table, and everyone looks up at me. "Sorry. I didn't mean to do that." I slide into the seat and pop the top on my Diet Coke.

"Er, are you okay there, Lillian?" Delilah has warmed up to me a lot, but I still feel like she resents the time Jensen spends with me.

"Yeah, sorry. I have to leave soon to head to my father's. There is a party this weekend I have to attend. It's a political thing." I poke at the food on my tray.

"Well, parties can be fun, right? You've got to be there all weekend?" I appreciate Delilah's attempt to spin it, but there is no way to put this in a positive light.

"Parties can be, sure, but these are always guaranteed to be awful. Anyway, what are you all doing this weekend?" Jensen sets his tray down next to me and pulls his chair out. "I'm golfing with Dad tomorrow, and if I am not mistaken, we have practice before lunch at Abuela's. You'll be back in time for that, right?"

"I'm supposed to be. If I am lucky, Father will be too hungover to care, and I can sneak out first thing." I sigh, pushing my tray away. "I can't do this. I'm not hungry. I'm just going to go and get this over with. I'll see you all on Sunday." I bus my tray before heading out to the parking lot.

"Angel baby!" Jensen jogs out after me. Are you okay? I've never seen you like this." I sigh. I know I'm acting off, but how can I explain to Jensen, with his perfect dad, that the thought of being in my father's presence makes me want to jump off a bridge?

"I know. I'm sorry. I am just not looking forward to this weekend." I shove my hair off my neck. It's hot outside, and I am more than ready to be in the AC of my car.

"Then don't go. Stay home with me and come to practice." Jensen pulls me closer, but I deliberately take a step back. "I can't. That's not an option. The functions with Father are never an option. They're a requirement. I have to go. I'll see you Sunday." I wrench open the car door, crank the car, and then the AC goes up to high. Once I can touch the steering wheel, I put the car in reverse and pull out of my parking space. Jensen stands there and watches me leave with a hurt look on his face, which makes me want to cry. I can't tell him. I want to, but he won't understand, and I can't let anyone know. If I don't go, then it all goes away. I made a deal with the devil and this is his due.

When I pull into the drive at the governor's mansion, I see all the cars in the driveway and know I am late for dinner. I exit the car and head up the broad steps into the foyer. I can hear the sounds of silverware, so I head straight for the formal dining room. I walk in with an apology ready, but I stop short at the addition of two people I don't recognize at the table. The older man looks foreign, with dark hair and rugged, tan skin. His bright green eyes meet mine, and he smirks. The younger man sitting next to him is clearly his son. They look the same, and there is something about both of them that reminds me of a shark. The conversation grinds to an abrupt halt.

"Ah, Lillian. Finally. Take your seat. I have some people I want you to meet." I slide into my appointed chair while Father continues. "This is Vincent and Marco Russo. Vincent owns Elite Auto Shine—a new car detailing business that just opened up in town—but he has branches all over the country. He made a very generous contribution to my campaign. He will be a guest of honor at the campaign party tomorrow. Young Marco is starting his first year at McCombs School of Business at the University of Texas in Austin. He plans to follow in his father's footsteps. Doesn't that sound amazing?"

"Oh. Yes, that does sound amazing. Congratulations, Marco." I place my napkin in my lap, and a maid brings out my plate. I look down at the meager offering and choke back a sigh. The bland chicken breast and asparagus on my plate look anything but appetizing. Michael was supposed to make fried catfish tonight with homemade tartar sauce. Once again, I wish to be anywhere but at this table.

"So, Lillian, your father tells me you saved a dance for me tomorrow night," Marco says.

I can feel his gaze on me as I stare at my plate. "Oh. Yes, of course. I have saved you a dance." I glance up at my father to see him watching me closely.

"Fantastic. I look forward to it."

Clarissa quickly monopolizes the remainder of the meal, discussing wedding plans and blatantly flirting with Vincent. This weekend may be the death of me.

Chapter Fifteen

Jensen

We're loading up the truck with clubs bright and early Saturday morning. I take a sip of my travel coffee mug and slam the tailgate. The absence of Lily last night was torture. We missed the latest episode of *Game of Thrones*, but she promised to catch up with me on Sunday night. I shoot her another text, but it stays unread. Whatever is going on at her father's house is keeping her busy. She has not answered my texts since leaving the school parking lot yesterday. I would be worried if I weren't sure she had made it, but she texted her mom that she arrived, so I know she is safely there. Dad climbs into the truck, and we head to the course. Even though it is early, several cars are in the lot, and groups are queueing up to start. We play a few holes before Dad finally breaks the silence.

"So what's going on, son?" I kick the ground, unsure if I want to open this can of worms. "Is it bad? Is Delilah pregnant? Whatever it is, you can tell me."

"Is Delilah *what*?" I'm so shocked, I miss my swing and my club flies down the fairway. "Dad, no. It isn't like that. I have told you that. I just... what... why?"

"Well, what am I supposed to think? You spend all your time together, you travel constantly, and you two have been inseparable since we moved here." Dad throws up his hands, and we walk down to retrieve my club.

"Dad, she loves someone else, not me, and I don't love her, so it's fine. I wanted to talk about Lily. What do you know about her dad and how she ended up with him and not Gwen?"

"Well, that's not an easy story, and frankly, it isn't mine to tell." Dad scratches the back of his neck. "I know I can tell you that her father fought for custody and threatened to drag Gwen through the mud if she tried to keep Lily. She wanted to put up more of a fight, but she was starting over with nothing and he is the governor, so they came to an 'understanding' about Lily. It was all done out of court, since he wanted to keep it out of the press. She moved to Riverbend, where we met. The rest you kind of already know. Why are you asking?"

I line up my shot again and take it, and the ball flies down the fairway to land on the rough. "Well, I kinda overheard bits and pieces of a conversation she had with him. She said he had her working with a personal trainer, dietitian, stylist, and many other things. She's already so tiny; I wouldn't say I like the idea of him making her lose weight. It can't be healthy."

"Well. I can't speak about how another parent chooses to raise their child. Still, I can watch her while she is with us and ensure she feels safe and secure enough to self-regulate her food consumption." I start to interrupt, but Dad holds up a hand.

"We can't make her do things she doesn't want to do; it has to be her choice, and by providing the options for her to make those choices, we are already doing more than it seems her father is. Let her enjoy the freedom that gives her while she's with us. That's the best thing we can do. I will also talk with Gwen, but she is reluctant to discuss anything about the governor. I think she thinks she's protecting me or something."

"Does that not seem odd to you, Dad? She is so afraid of this guy that she doesn't want to mention him?" I'm agitated, thinking my angel baby is around this man alone and without protection.

"Well, bud, there are people in this world who are not good, and sometimes you don't realize it until it is too late. That's why all we can do is try to be the best possible person and stay kind. Everyone you meet is fighting a battle, whether you know it or not. One kind word or action can change everything for a person in distress."

"Yeah, Dad. That's what you've always told me. It's also why we donate to charity and volunteer at the homeless shelters."

Dad claps me on the shoulder again before pulling me into a side hug. "That's right, bud. We are more fortunate than others and should always do what we can to help those less fortunate. Now, do you feel better?" I nod, and he ruffles my hair. "Good. Now, let's finish these nine holes and head home. Gwen was going to Riverbend to pick up some breakfast pastries."

When we are packing to head home, the clubhouse is busy with golfers milling around the waiting golf carts.

"Michael?" a voice calls out, and we turn to see Mr. Stone walking up. "I thought that was you. How have you been? Grayson has been telling us the good news. Is the band getting the agent's attention? What do you make of all that?"

Dad swings his clubs into the truck's bed before shaking hands with Mr. Stone. "Well, I think it is amazing. We knew they had the talent, and this just reinforces that. I helped Delilah do some research the other day and field some requests. She's narrowed it down to three different ones she will invite to view some shows."

Mr. Stone raises his eyebrows. "Delilah did, huh? Did she talk to anyone else about it?"

Dad rolls his eyes. "She talked to me about it, and then the kids had a meeting, and she made the phone calls the next day. Of course they reached out to her first; she's the face of the band. However, the agreement on who to invite involved all members."

Mr. Stone blusters for a moment, seemingly trying to make excuses for being an ass when it comes to Delilah. She may be bold and loud and in your face, but she is also one of the best friends I have ever had, and she would give the shirt off her back to help someone she cares for.

"We all talked about it, Mr. Stone. Grayson included. He brought up some crucial questions that we need to ask, and we all agreed on who to invite after reviewing the information about the labels." I grab the keys from Dad and hit the remote start button. It may only be ten a.m., but it is ten a.m. in Texas, and it is already pushing 80° F. I don't want to spend half the ride home cooking my ass on hot leather seats. "Have a good game, Mr. Stone." I climb into the truck and shut the door for the rest of the conversation. Mr. Stone likes to pretend he is invested in his son. But you only have to watch him attempt to sign to Grayson for a minute to realize that his interest is only surface level.

Dad gets in the truck a few moments later and shakes his head before backing out. "That man makes me want to scream whenever I speak with him. I have no doubt he loves his son, but he can't wait for him to be out of the house."

"I thought I was the only one who thought that. Grayson says he's never said anything to him and has always given him whatever he needed for his music but spends more time with his siblings than with him." Dad hums in the back of his throat as we turn back down Main Street, headed to our house. "I think I will go over and see what Delilah is up to after breakfast. Is that okay?"

Chuckling, Dad pulls into our driveway. "Son, you practically lived there until recently. I think we both know it is more than okay. Tell me if you won't be coming home, and be safe and have fun."

I jump out of the truck and head for the front door. "I'm still going to get some of those pastries! Delilah can't boil water, and Ms. C works weekends!" Dad laughs as we head into the house.

"Well, it sounds like you two had fun!" Gwen is sitting at the counter sipping a cup of coffee, and a plate of kolaches and apple fritters is in front of her. Dad kisses her on the cheek and snags a fritter. "Oh, we did. I played a respectable forty-nine. Jensen was just behind me with a fifty-five."

Gwen chuckles. "I don't know what those numbers mean, but I am glad you had fun. What else is on the agenda for today?"

I slide around and grab a couple of kolaches and fritters, putting them in a Ziplock. "I'm afraid you two are on your own. I am heading over to Delilah's to see what's going on and get some extra practice. The scout from Revelation Records is coming next weekend to watch us play at the 4H auction, and we want to nail down the setlist."

I hug Dad, and Gwen holds her fist up for a bump as I grab my guitar and head out the door. I shove half of a kolache in my mouth, knowing Delilah will want the fritter with her twentieth cup of coffee for the morning. I text Lily a good morning before slipping behind the wheel and driving the two streets to Delilah's house. An hour later, we are halfway through the first run-through of our set list. I completely forget about checking my phone after that, too distracted by the music.

Chapter Sixteen

Lily

I check my phone for the 500th time this morning. I just got out of the shower when I got the good morning text from Jensen. I had about ten minutes before the hairstylist arrived, so I quickly shot him a text back, only to be met with silence. The message didn't even show as read. Now the hairstylist is here, and I am in the middle of a transformation: high light, low lights, trimmed, glossed, and shined up like a new penny. I have a manicurist and a pedicurist working on getting my hands and toes to an acceptable appearance. My stylist will be here later with a selection of gowns—already pre-approved by Father—for me to pick from. I just wanted a few minutes with Jensen before dealing with all of this.

Having Vincent and Marco at dinner last night threw me. Something about them doesn't feel right even though they were both perfect gentlemen. I can't believe Father said I would dance with Marco tonight, but I know better than to refuse. I sigh and settle back into the chair, my mind wandering. What is Jensen doing right now? He was supposed to play golf with Michael, but surely that doesn't take all morning?

"How long does it take to play a round of golf?" I wonder out loud.

"It can take up to four hours if you play the full eighteen holes." I jump, and the manicurist apologizes. "I'm sorry, miss. I thought you wanted an answer."

I shake my head. "Oh, no. Don't apologize. I did want an answer. I just hadn't realized I had spoken out loud." She smiles at me before going back to my nails. Classic French tip. Typical. Father wouldn't have chosen anything else, even though Clarissa could potentially kill a man with the claws she typically wears. No one would even know because they are always blood red. I hear her laughter going down the hall and past my room as if on cue. Rolling my eyes, I lean back in the chair and daydream about magnolia trees and a pasture that extends as far as you can see.

Lunch is melon, prosciutto, and yogurt with chia seeds. I eat my meager fair before lying down to nap. Father always insists on taking a nap before anything campaign related. I have two hours, then I will be given the final touches, zipped into an uncomfortable tulle creation, and paraded around like a prized horse.

I hear the hum of conversation as I head down the stairs to join the party. People started showing up early. Father will be thrilled. I snag a glass of champagne off the sideboard and step behind a curtain to take a drink before setting it down on the corner of a shelf. Dom Pérignon, typical. I am positive Father gets it delivered by the case during an election year. I skirt around the party's edge, the silver-white of the dress making it hard to hide in the shadows.

"Lillian, I was hoping I would find you. You look lovely tonight." Marco Russo steps in from the balcony.

"Marco. Hello. Thank you. You look very dashing in your tux." He shrugs a shoulder before cupping my elbow and moving us toward our fathers. "Oh, I was just about to..." I gesture back toward the balcony, but he doesn't let my elbow go, deftly steering us through the crowd.

"Your father was looking for you. Let us speak with him, and then we can have that dance, hmmm?" Before I can protest anymore, we are in front of my father and Vincent, who turn to greet me.

"Good evening. It is lovely to see you again, Mr. Russo. Father." I glance around the room at the people present. I see the mayor and his wife chatting with the president of UT Austin and his husband. Several board members are drinking scotch and chatting over the hors d'oeuvres.

"Lillian?" I turn my attention back to Vincent and blanch when I realize I have been addressed several times but didn't realize it.

"I am so sorry. I was gathering butterflies and didn't realize you were talking to me. How very rude. Could you please repeat the question?"

Vincent smiles. "I simply asked if you were looking forward to attending Wellesley. Your father mentioned that was your plan after high school."

"Oh, yes. I am very excited to be attending. It is a lovely school, and I am fortunate to have been accepted so early." It's easy to be accepted when your father pays off the admissions officer; however, I don't say that out loud.

"Maybe you and Marco should go have that dance now," my father says, and I smile at him before accepting Marco's hand.

"That would be lovely. Thank you." Marco pulls me close, and we waltz around the room silently for a few minutes.

"You know. I will intern in New York with my uncle Salvatore after I graduate." I smile but don't comment as Marco begins to ramble about everything he's been learning about his father's business. I almost miss it when he adds, "I could take you out sometime."

"That would be love—wait, I am sorry—what?" I shake my head. The champagne must have gotten to me because I cannot concentrate this evening.

"When we have both graduated? I said maybe I could take you out for dinner one night."

I stare at him for a few minutes, stumbling over a polite way to say over my dead fucking body, but what comes out is, "Oh, but I am going to be in Boston while you're in New York. If you find yourself in Boston, we can see about that then. Of course." Marco smiles and spins me out and back as the music ends. I smile back and thank him before doing my best to get lost in the crowd. I can hide for the rest of the evening if I am lucky. I know one thing for sure. I will never go on a date with Marco Russo. Not in a million years.

The sun has barely breached the horizon when I climb into my car. Everyone in the house is still sleeping off the effects of overindulgence. Father won't be pleased I left without staying for another lecture, but he was more than happy with me last night, so I am willing to take my chances. Right now, I only care about getting back to Havenbrook and Jensen. I turn on my favorite playlist and let the highway lead me home. I have the freeway to myself for most of the drive, my only companions being the occasional eighteen-wheeler. Thanks to the lack of traffic, I pull up to the house at about eight a.m. and notice that Jensen's truck isn't here. I sit in my car momentarily, confusion and sadness warring in my chest. He knew I was supposed to be back first thing this morning. We made plans.

I get out of my car, digging my house keys out of my bag. The house is quiet when I open the door. The morning sun shines into the kitchen, and I can see a note addressed to me propped on the fruit bowl. Tossing my keys on the entry table, I pick up the note; the handwriting on the front says it's from Mom. Opening the envelope, I read that Mom and Michael went to Houston and will be back this afternoon. At least someone remembered I would be home this morning. So I am home alone. I stare around the room again, and the déjà vu from my initial night in this house strikes me. What is the matter with me that keeps me ending up alone? I toss the letter on the bar before heading to my room. At least I can shower and sleep more than a few hours.

I feel someone tucking my hair behind my ear, and a smile spreads across my lips. I know that scent anywhere. "Jensen," I murmur without opening my eyes. "You're home."

He brushes my cheek. "Yeah, angel baby, I'm sorry I wasn't here when you arrived. I was at practice with Delilah, and we crashed around three a.m. No excuses, though."

I sit up, seeing Jensen kneeling by my bed. "You were with Delilah all night?" I know they're best friends, but how often he stays at her place is strange.

Jensen gives me a look. "Yeah, we were practicing. Some talent scouts are coming to shows soon, and we need to be on top of our game."

I shove my hair from my face as I reach for my robe. "Oh. Okay."

Jensen isn't buying it. "Angel baby, what's wrong?"

I struggle with my sleeve and huff in frustration. "It's nothing. It's fine. Don't worry about it."

Jensen takes the robe, fixes the sleeve, and helps me into it. "Angel baby, when a woman says it's fine, it's anything but. Why don't you tell me what's bothering you so we can deal with it and get ready for lunch at Abuela's?"

Chapter Seventeen

Jensen

I can tell right away I messed up. I've never seen that look on Lily's face, but I've seen it on Delilah's, and I know I fucked up. I raise my hands in surrender and step back. "I could've phrased that better. I'm sorry. I haven't had coffee yet, and my brain-to-mouth filter isn't working." Lily glares at me, and I take another step back.

"I said nothing is wrong. Please leave the room so I can get dressed." She points at her bedroom door, and I glare at the offending finger.

"No. I won't leave until you tell me what's wrong. I've done something to upset you."

"Well, why don't I go over to Marco's house, spend the night, and then come home the next morning acting like it's perfectly okay?"

I see red at her words and stalk toward her until she's backed against the wall. "Who is Marco, and why do you want to spend the night at his house?"

I can see her pulse thrumming at the base of her neck, and I can't stop myself from burying my face in that spot. "Marco is the son of one of my father's campaign contributors. I met him at dinner on Friday and saw him again at the party last night. I don't want to spend the night at his house, but it isn't any different for me than you so casually spending the night at Delilah's. I know you say you're just friends and jealousy isn't attractive, but I am jealous because I know we may never do that."

I pull her close so we are pressed together as tightly as possible. "Oh, angel baby. You have no reason to be jealous. I promise. If it makes you feel better, I will ensure I don't spend the night at Delilah's anymore."

Lily looks up at me, her bright blue eyes shining in the morning light, and I can't help it. I brush my lips against hers, and her lips part as she gasps against mine. I gaze intently at her but take a chance and kiss her again. It takes a minute for us to get the positions of our faces right, but when we do, I can't slow down. It is like an inferno has started and only her lips can quench it. I slide my tongue against her bottom lip, and she opens, our tongues fumbling, desperate for more. When she stands on tiptoe, trying to get closer, I pick her up, and her legs automatically lock around my waist. I break the kiss, and we pant for air.

"Angel baby." Lily lunges up, sliding against me until her lips are pressed to mine again, her hands in my hair. I have one arm supporting her under her ass, and my other slides up her side until I can feel her warm skin. I groan in my throat. "Angel baby, tell me to stop. Tell me to stop, and I will walk away right now. Tell me." I am practically pleading with her at this point. The last thing I want to do is something she doesn't like.

Lily's lips are swollen, and her pupils are blown so wide that only a thin ring of blue is still visible. Lily rocks against me, and I groan out loud. I have never been this turned on in my entire life. "Don't stop." Her words shock me into action, gripping her tighter and spinning to lay her on the bed, wedging myself between her legs. I slam my lips back down onto hers, nipping her bottom lip. We have the rhythm now. My dick is so hard I am afraid I will embarrass myself as I rock against her. Lily whines, her hips rocking up to meet mine.

We're both fumbling and unsure but are so turned on we don't care. I manage to shove her pajama top up, and I am greeted by two pink, perky nipples attached to more than a generous handful of the most beautiful breasts I have seen in my life. I lick a nipple, and Lily gasps as I pull it into my mouth, tonguing it and sucking.

Lily bucks up hard against me, and I use my hips to push her back down onto the bed. She's grabbing and clawing at my hair at this point. I take both sides of her top and rip it open, buttons flying all over the room. With the top out of the way, I grab her wrists and pin them to the bed so that I can worship her nipples without losing all of my hair.

Lily is soaking wet, and it is starting to coat my jeans. Groaning, I reach down and pop the button on them, giving my cock some room. Lily's hand follows mine, delving in to wrap her small hand around me. With a choked shout, I bite down harder on her nipple as I start to come. With Lily's hand gripping me, I thrust against her over and over again until she cries out, her body arching under mine. We lay there for several minutes as our heart rates try to return to normal. I kiss her lips softly, and she smiles at me, her body soft and pliant against mine. I roll us and tug her close until she is cuddled against my side.

I'm not sure how long we lay there, but eventually, I start to move. "Angel baby, we need to get cleaned up." Lily groans, and I smile. I kiss the top of her head, and she stares up at me, her lips still swollen and her hair a tangled mess around her head. "Are you okay with what happened?" I can feel a lump form in my throat. I might die if she says no, but she just blushes and nods, and the breath I was holding rushes out. "Good. That was amazing, angel baby. You're amazing. Let's get you into the shower, c'mon."

We both stand, Lily's cheeks flushing pink as she holds her ruined top together. "Here." I grab a pair of jeans and a button-up from her closet and hand them to her. "Go shower. I'll meet you back here in twenty." I brush a soft kiss on her forehead and head to my room. Grabbing a dirty shirt from the floor, I clean up the mess I made on my stomach and kick off my jeans. While Lily is in the shower, I get dressed before heading back into her room to crack the windows. The last thing I need is for our parents to come home and find her room smells like what we were doing. I straighten her comforter and arrange her pillows before grabbing some juice in the kitchen. Gulping down the first cup, I refill it and head to sit on the couch until Lily is done with her shower.

She walks out of her room fifteen minutes later, but she's not meeting my eyes. Striding over to her, I tilt her chin. "You alright there, angel baby?" She shrugs her shoulder. "That's not an answer." I pull her closer, resting her head against my chest. "I don't regret anything we did, angel baby; if anything, I regret that we have to go to Abuela's." Lily's stomach takes that moment to growl, and I chuckle. "Well, maybe we should get going, if your stomach has anything to say about it." Lily smiles up at me from her spot on my chest. I kiss the tip of her nose before pulling her toward the front door. "Let's go get something to eat, and then we can come back here and watch *Game of Thrones.*"

I am in the process of settling her in the truck when she breaks the silence. "Thank you. I don't know what happened earlier. I was feeling shy, I guess. I haven't ever done anything remotely like that before, but just being around you makes me feel better."

I smile at her and buckle her seat belt. "Lily, haven't you figured it out yet?" At her confused look, I cup her face. "There isn't much I wouldn't do to ensure you were happy and comfortable." At that declaration, I climb into the driver's seat and head to Abuela's house. The number of vehicles parked outside the house gives a glimpse into the chaos inside.

I park the truck before turning to Lily. "Looks like it is going to be a full house. I want you to listen to me. The minute—no, the second—you are ready to go, you say something, and we go. Do you understand?" Lily nods, her blue eyes wide at the sheer number of vehicles. "It will be crazy, but I can promise you some amazing food." When her stomach grumbles again, I chuckle before heading to help her out of the truck. I grab her hand and tug her up weathered stairs, the screen door slamming open as a handful of kids run out of the house screaming and laughing. Walking out of the oppressive heat and into the relative coolness of the house is a short reprieve before the spice-laden air slaps us in the face.

"Abuela! We're here!" The women are in the kitchen speaking rapid-fire Spanish back and forth over all the pots and pans that hold lunch. The men are either watching the football game, drinking beer, or around the pit outside, which I know will probably have a goat or two roasting on it. I start pointing out the ones Lily hasn't met yet and introducing them to her. Cousins, aunts, uncles, nephews and nieces, they are all in at-tendance.

Abuela bustles out of the kitchen, wiping her hands on her apron and putting a giant smile on her crinkled face. "Mijito! You made it, and you brought Lily! How wonderful!" I am pulled into a crushing hug, and I have to smile at the feeling. Before moving to Havenbrook, I couldn't remember when someone other than Dad hugged me. "Now, Lily, have you ever made carne asada? No? Come. I'll show you." Lily looks frantically back at me as Abuela leads her into the kitchen, but I just smile.

I snag her other hand, pulling her back toward me. "Abuela, I'm going to show Lily around the house. Maybe she could join you and the other ladies another time?"

Chapter Eighteen

Lily

By the time I finished my shower, I thought I was about to have a panic attack. I wasn't prepared for what happened between Jensen and me, nor did I regret it. I have never felt anything like that in my life. So by the time I made my way back to the living room, I was feeling so shy I didn't know if I could function at lunch, but then Jensen knew just what to do and say to put me at ease.

Getting to Abuela's house though, my anxiety was back at seeing all the cars and people. Abuela has been welcoming the few times I have interacted with her, but I didn't expect her to try to kidnap me to the kitchen to help cook! The most I can do is avocado toast and a lovely Earl Grey Tea! Luckily, Jensen managed to steal me back.

We're heading up the stairs to a long hallway. Jensen keeps a steady stream of chatter going about family members and funny anecdotes. We stop outside one closed door. "This was Dad's room growing up. It's the room I stay in sometimes if I spend the night." He opens the door, and we enter a room with blue-painted walls, baseball prints, and culinary cookbooks scattered throughout.

I head over to the dresser and pick up a framed picture of Jensen and his dad where they are sitting on the front porch. I pick it up and study it, but the door clicking behind me has me turning. Jensen locks the door, and his long legs eat up the space between us. "I have been thinking about this ever since we got here." He slants his lips over mine, and we find our way quickly this time. Jensen's hand slides up into my hair to cup the back of my head, and I slide my hands up his chest to wrap around his neck. When he pulls away, breathing heavily, I stretch up, eager for more. He meets me halfway, and the dresser is pressing painfully into my back, but I don't care. Jensen's lips are on mine, and my world feels complete again. His other hand slides up and massages my breast, and I swear that stars explode in my head. It feels so amazing, I don't want to stop. I want to keep going, and from the sounds coming from Jensen, he wants to also.

A sudden banging and raucous laughter from downstairs has us jumping apart. Jensen heads back to lean against the door, and I grip the dresser behind me, panting heavily. Jensen tucks his shirt back in before walking over and adjusting my clothes back to where they were. "C'mon, angel baby. Let's get back downstairs. Apparently, it isn't safe for us up here." He smirks when he says it, so I know he isn't truly complaining.

I grin back before taking his hand and following him down the stairs. In the short time we were upstairs, the dining room table has become laden with various dishes. Everything is served buffet style, and I can't help but marvel at the sheer amount of food that has been prepared. Short of a campaign party or inaugural ball, I have never seen so much food.

"Don't worry, we can go down the line together, and I will tell you what each dish is."

Well, that takes care of one worry; the second, and one that Jensen can't so quickly quell, is how I am going to eat even a third of the dishes on this table! "Why is there so much food? Are we expecting more people?" That could be it. Perhaps some people are still on the way to help consume the abundance before me.

Jensen chuckles. "There are usually some late stragglers, but I can promise there will barely be any leftovers after this bunch gets through with it. Now, let's wait for the tide to slow, and we can set you up."

"Now, Lily, tell me, what do you do for fun?" Abuela is sitting across from me. Her brown eyes, while kind, are still sharp as ever.

"Oh. Well. I don't really know. I guess I like to watch TV? I haven't really had a chance to do much outside of school. I was on the volleyball team at my old school for a while, but then I had to drop out. I kept missing practices and games due to attending my father's events. It was fun while I was on the team, though. Oh, I also like to go running."

Jensen grins in glee. "I didn't know you used to play volleyball! That's awesome! I bet you were amazing."

I grin back but shrug a shoulder. "I was okay."

"Surely you have something else you like to do? *Mijito*, he has his band, and my Michael has his cooking."

I shake my head. I don't have anything like that; the closest thing I had was obsession with a person, not a hobby. "I'm afraid not. There weren't many opportunities for things like that at my boarding school."

Abuela tuts. "Well, it is a good thing you are here now, yes? We can help you find your passion." Abuela speaks as though her word is law, and everything I know about the woman says that that is precisely how it is. I doubt anyone in their right mind would disagree with Abuela. Not if they knew what was good for them.

As we sit there eating and chatting, I see people getting up for second and third helpings while I try to make my way through my first. Jensen gave me a little bit of everything since I had no idea what any of the dishes were and we were holding up the line with him trying to explain each one. I was a massive fan of the carne asada, but not so much of the menudo. I didn't even ask what I was supposed to be eating. The look of it was enough to put me off the rest of my lunch. I pick at my plate, happy to let the conversation flow around me, a hodgepodge of English and

Spanish. Someone hollers something in Spanish from the living room. Jensen answers, his tone aggressive, and the conversation dies as the crowd waits.

I look across the room to see who spoke, but there are too many people, and I am too short. Jensen stands, scraping his chair across the floor loudly in the silence. "*Di eso una vez más, te reto.*" Jensen's tone is deadly, and his posture is aggressive. No one says a word as he matches eyes with whoever is on the other side of the living room.

"*¡Todos, basta! ¡Esta es mi casa y me respetarán en mi casa! ¡Si no están de acuerdo, pueden irse y no regresar!*" Abuela stands in the kitchen doorway, every bit the matriarch of her family. She places the plate of cookies on the table, her steps slow and even. "Have you lost your minds? Do you behave like this in this house? How dare you!" I'm looking around at all the hanging heads, and I am in awe of the presence Abuela projects. "*Fernando, vete.*" Fernando stands up and slinks out the back door. I recognize him as one of Jensen's cousins.

"Now, everyone. Dessert! Jensen, *mijito, siéntate.* Lilita, have you tried my pan de polvo?" I take the small plate of cookies and smile at her. Abuela pats my cheeks as Jensen sits back down, so close to me I can feel the heat radiating off him.

He leans closer to whisper in my ear. "Are you done eating?" I nod my head. I am so full I am starting to get sleepy, and he smiles as I yawn. "Let's get you home, I think you may need a nap." He chuckles when I grumble, but he's not exactly wrong.

The whole way home, I do my best to get Jensen to tell me what Fernando said, but he refuses. We're still arguing about it when we walk in the front door. "You are so damn stubborn, Jensen Parker! You can't protect me from everything!" Jensen snorts before heading to the kitchen to grab me a bottle of cherry-flavored sparkling water.

"I may not be able to protect you from everything, but I can protect you from this. Drop it, angel baby. It isn't going to happen. C'mon, let's go get comfortable and watch *Game of Thrones*."

I huff and flop down on the couch. Jensen fluffs up a bunch of pillows, making sure I am comfortable. He grabs the remote and the couch blanket, spreading it over my legs. He turns on the TV and goes to pull up the latest episode. As I am sucked into the world of White Walkers, Jon Snow, and Castle Black, I can feel my eyelids getting heavier and heavier. Before I know it, I'm sound asleep.

Chapter Nineteen

Jensen

I sit on the couch, watching Lily sleep. *Game of Thrones* plays in the background, but I can't be bothered enough to follow the episode. All I can think about is hunting down Fernando and punching his teeth down his throat. He has always been annoying, and it seems he has yet to improve. I breathe in through my nose and out through my mouth like my therapist taught me to help manage my temper. Just about the time I think I have it under control, I glance at Lily's sleeping face, innocent and beautiful in the afternoon light, and I want to throttle Fernando all over again.

I hear the keys in the lock, and Dad and Gwen walk into the house. I hold a finger to my mouth, shushing them before they wake Lily. Gwen peeks over the couch and smiles. "The drive always did wear her out." Dad motions me into the kitchen, and I make my way gingerly off the sofa to follow. "Bud, Abuela called me and told me about what happened at lunch." For a moment, the bottom of my stomach drops to my knees. What was Dad told? "I know he's annoying, but you can't beat Fernando." I blink at him in shock. Fernando. Of course.

"Dad—"

He shakes his head. "No, Jensen. You know as well as I do, the moment you start something with Fernando, Enrique will get involved, and it's better for everyone that that does not happen."

I release a frustrated breath. "Fine. I won't do anything about it. Besides, I don't think Fernando is brave enough to buck up. He's still smarting from when I whipped his ass at Christmas."

Dad chuckles. "Be that as it may, I need you to promise me that you won't go looking for Fernando and stirring up trouble."

We hook pinkies. "Promise."

Since I missed most of the episode, I swap the channel to ESPN to see if I can catch some scores, and I browse VidReel on my phone. It looks like Wild Child Reckless is trending again. Delilah must have uploaded a new video. Swapping over to our page, I see I need to do some cleanup. Ever since we started getting popular on the app, the number of perverts making derogatory remarks about Delilah has doubled. Delilah's brother, James, and I do our best to delete and block most comments before Delilah can see them. Glancing at a sleeping Lily, I remember her remarks about spending the night at Marcos's house. She's never mentioned Marco before. I file the name in the back of my mind to check on later.

When Lily stirs an hour later, I put my phone away and move to push her hair behind her ear once again. "Good morning, sunshine." She grins at me, and I grin back. "Do you feel like going out tonight?"

Lily wrinkles her nose. "Tonight? It's a school night."

I chuckle—my little rule follower. "I promise we won't be out late. There was talk about the twins having a party in their dad's pasture. Wild Child Reckless will usually play a song or two. If you don't want to go, we don't have to. It was just a thought."

"I don't think I have anything appropriate to wear." She nibbles on her bottom lip, and I can only think about kissing them again.

Clearing my throat, I pull her up off the couch. "Well, let's go check." I'm flipping through her closet while she sits on her bed. I pull out a pair of jeans and a tank top. "Try these on for me." Lily shoots me a shy look before slipping into the bathroom to change. While she is changing, I run to my room to grab my pocketknife.

"What do you think?" Lily stands nervously before me.

"Are you attached to the jeans?"

She looks at me like I've lost my mind. "No, I guess not more than my other jeans." I kneel in front of her and flick open my pocketknife. "Jensen! What are you—" Before she can finish the sentence, I start cutting her jeans off about mid-thigh. Lily squeals, trying to stay still since my knife is still next to her legs. "Jensen! These are designer jeans!"

I shrug. "You said you weren't attached to them and didn't think you had anything to wear to the party. Now you do." I grab a pair of black and gray boots with butterflies stitched into the leather. They're gorgeous and new, and the leather smell is still rich. "Put these on. I'm going to go change and grab my guitar."

We load up quickly, and I text Delilah that we are headed that way. Swinging by her house, I help her load up the rest of the gear. Grayson pulls up right as we are getting ready to head out. I wave for him to follow us, and we head to the Thompson twins' pasture. The party is in full swing by the time we get there, and I spot a keg out two scattered around. I back up to the half barn, and Delilah jumps out of the truck, acting like she's been cooped up for a million years. I shake my head at Grayson, and I move to unload the trucks.

"Delilah, why do you two get us some drinks while we do this? Also, we *will* have a strict list this time." Delilah sticks her tongue out at me before heading to grab drinks. Lily follows behind her, answering the questions Delilah is peppering her with. The girl can't shut up to save her life.

We start playing soon after, and the more Delilah drinks, the wilder the set gets. She keeps the crowd dancing and drinking for hours. It has been a great way to blow off steam and try out new covers. Even Lily seems to be having fun, her cheeks flushed and her eyes bright with alcohol. We launch into a Taylor Swift cover. This one has me singing along with Delilah. Where I would typically play off Delilah, this time I gaze firmly at Lily. Delilah notices and looks at me weirdly, but I pretend I don't see. There is only one girl for me now, and I want her to know it.

We play several sets that night, and I take plenty of breaks to spend time with Lily. Grayson shakes his head at us before starting to pack up his kit. We high-five before he heads out, and he hugs Lily, laughing at the look on my face. Grabbing Lily's hand, I lead her away from the front, and she smiles as she follows me.

"Where are we going?" She's not drunk, but she's definitely on the far side of sober. I chuckle and keep walking.

"I have something I want to show you. Just up here on the hill." Reaching the top of the hill, I pull Lily in front of me, wrapping my arms around her waist. "Look up." Lily looks up and gasps. The light pollution barely exists this far from the fire, and the night sky stretches before us like a blanket.

"There is the Big Dipper. There is the Little Dipper. My dad always called that one the Three Sisters, but it's Orion's Belt."

Lily sways in my arms, her eyes reflecting the stars back at me. "I've never seen the stars like this. It's so beautiful, Jensen. Thank you."

I sit down on the ground and pull her down with me to sit in between my legs. I'm unsure how long we sit there just staring at the stars decorating the night sky. Eventually, Lily starts to yawn. "C'mon, angel baby. Let's get you back home and in bed."

By the time we return to my truck, Grayson has loaded my kit and grabbed Delilah. I text him thanks and load Lily up in my truck. She's sound asleep by the time we exit the pasture, and I spend the ride home glancing at her sleeping face. She's so damn pretty it hurts to look at her sometimes. But it's also like, if I don't, she could disappear. Pulling up to the house, she doesn't stir when I kill the engine. Slipping out, I walk up to unlock and open the door before heading back and picking her up out of the cab. Lily sighs and rests her head on my shoulder. Smiling, I head to her room and lay her on the bed, removing her boots. I cover her with a throw blanket from the bottom of her bed and ensure she's as comfortable as possible.

I head out to bring in my kit and lock up the house. I grab a bottle of water and some aspirin and place them on Lily's bedside table. I doubt she drank enough to be hungover, but it's better to be safe than sorry. I put down a bottle myself before heading to bed. I stare at the ceiling for hours, replaying the last few days. As it always does when I think about Lily, I can feel my body responding and groan. Knowing I won't be getting any sleep, I reach down and grip my shaft. I start slowly, replaying the feel of Lily's nipples in my mouth. My hand speeds up when I think about the sounds she made while my mouth was on her. My breath is rasping in and out of my lungs, and I swear I may go up in flames. Then I remember the sounds she made as she fell apart under me, and it's over. Choking back a cry, I spill all over my stomach, the muscles trembling as the long ropes land. Panting, I lay there for a minute, waiting for the ability to move to return. When it does, I grab a dirty shirt off the floor and clean myself up. Rolling over, I drift off to sleep, my dreams filled with bright blue eyes and long blonde hair.

Chapter Twenty

Lily- Two Years Later

I spend the next two years in a euphoric bubble. Jensen stays busy with Wild Child Reckless, whose popularity is soaring. Revelation Records sent a contract that outshined the competition, so the band is moving to L.A. at the end of the year. Father got re-elected, which means fewer trips to the governor's mansion, but it also signals my dwindling freedom. While the band discusses labels, tours, and concerts, I pretend to be excited about school. I want to go with Jensen, choose my future, pursue my passions, and live on my own terms.

I'm leaving Chemistry when Delilah runs up. "Lils, I need to borrow Jensen. My truck still hasn't been replaced, and we're playing at the twins' on Friday night. I know you have that thing with your father, so I wanted to check if it's cool." Jensen and Delilah's easy friendship still surprises me, but they're just friends. The more I got to know Delilah, the more apparent it was that Alexander was her only focus. Jensen agrees but thinks it would take something significant for either of them to make a move.

"Hey, Dee, that's fine. I'm supposed to attend this press event, but I'm trying to use finals as an excuse. Father's pushing, though." That's putting it mildly—his recent texts demanded my attendance, with implied consequences I know all too well. I sigh as Delilah skips off to share the plan with Jensen.

"You know you're invited, right?" Jensen says, standing in front of me, his hazel eyes intent. I laugh. I haven't needed an invitation to a party since my second year at Havenbrook. If Jensen was going to be there, I would be too—come hell or high water, even if that water was governor shaped.

"You know I never miss a chance to see you perform. However, I am supposed to attend that press thing this weekend. So you are free to chauffer Delilah around to your heart's content."

Jensen grumbles. "I wouldn't have to if she hadn't totaled her truck."

I laugh and slap his arm. "Tell me what songs you will be playing so I can pretend I am there while eating salmon puffs and snacking on crudités."

Jensen loops an arm around my shoulder as we exit the school and enter the parking lot. Over the last two years, the casual affection Jensen shows me in public has ramped up; it's like the closer we get to graduation, the less of a fuck he gives about who says something. I love it. After years of sneaking around, it is liberating to be more openly affectionate. I was against it for so long, protesting every hand hold and chaste peck on my forehead. Then one day Jensen sat down with me, and when I expressed my very real fear about Father finding out he simply asked me if it made me happy and if I wanted to be happy. I realized then that, goddamn it, yes I did want to be happy! Since that day, I stopped fighting him so much on it.

"Delilah hasn't picked a set yet. We had a lot this week with setting up meetings with lawyers to review contracts, and my grandparents found out where we are."

Jensen never talks about that side of his family. It is like they don't exist. Our first big fight was about them. I have never seen Jensen as angry as I did that night. I cried myself to sleep only to wake up with him wrapped around me. We both apologized, and I promised never to bring them up again; the fact that he is bringing them up now is shocking.

"Wow. What do they want?"

Jensen's face turns to stone. "I don't know, and I don't care. They can burn in hell right alongside their daughter." I nod before pulling my car keys out of my pocket and remotely starting the car. One good thing about having a father obsessed with his image is having a brand new car every year with all the bells and whistles. Remote start in Texas is a godsend. The last thing anyone wants to do is burn their ass on hot leather seats.

We walk into the house and see Mom and Mike standing at the counter. "Lily-bean, come sit down." I swallow hard, feeling a ball of lead settle in my stomach. I perch on a stool, and Jensen stands behind me.

"What's going on?" I ask, looking between them.

Mom sighs. "I just got a call from your father. There was a bomb threat at the venue where he was supposed to speak. The event has been canceled."

I can't help the smile that spreads across my face. "That's great! I didn't want to go anyway! So what's the problem? Why do you both look so upset?"

Mike and Mom exchange a look. "Well, since you were supposed to be out of town this weekend and Jensen had band stuff, we booked a weekend getaway in Galveston."

I stare at them, confused. "Okay... that sounds lovely. I'm still not seeing a problem here."

Mom moves around the counter toward me. "We don't want to leave you here alone! We know you don't like it, and there's that storm coming in. But if we cancel now, we'll lose the deposit."

I take her hand. "Mom, it's fine. Go. I can hang out with Delilah and everyone else, and if I get scared, Jensen's here. He won't let anything happen to me."

Mom scans my face. "Are you sure?"

I smile reassuringly. "I'm sure. Go. Have fun. You deserve it."

Mom kisses my cheek. "I love you, Lily-bean."

Jensen chimes in, "That means you can come with us to the gig!"

Mike narrows his eyes. "What gig? I didn't know y'all had a gig planned this weekend."

Jensen hightails it to his room as Mike glares after him. Mom and I chuckle, and I grab my book bag and head to my bedroom. I'm not surprised to walk in and see Jensen waiting for me.

"You know, one of these days you're going to be waiting in here for me, and it's not going to be me who walks in."

Jensen chuckles darkly. "I doubt that, angel baby. You know what this means, right?"

I throw my bag onto my bed and pull out my Chemistry book. Even though finals are coming up, Mr. Downs is still assigning homework. That man needs a hobby. "What does what mean?"

I can feel the heat from his body as he presses up against my back to whisper in my ear. "It means you are all mine this weekend, angel baby." I can feel a shiver travel down my body. Jensen and I fool around when we can, but we still have not gone all the way. Last week during *Game of Thrones*, he used his hand on me; I nearly made my lip bleed, biting it, trying to stay quiet as he teased and tortured me until I fell apart.

"I'm always yours, Jensen." I can feel his hands sliding under the hem of my skirt, and I lean back against his shoulder.

"I'm glad you know that, angel baby, because I never plan on letting you go." He slides a finger under the edge of my panties, and I spread my legs in response. "However, I meant that since we will have the house to ourselves, I can do whatever I want." He kisses the side of my neck. "Whenever I want." He bites my ear lobe, and I have to stifle a moan. His finger slides through my folds, and I know I'm already slick. He uses the pad of his index finger to swirl around my clit before pulling back and kissing my temple. When I make a noise in protest, he just smiles at me. "Just wait, angel baby. I have just what you need." Kissing my nose, he heads to his room, shooting me a cheeky grin before shutting the door.

Collapsing into my desk chair, I stare at my Chemistry book wondering how I will concentrate on homework now. I glare at the closed door before flinging open my textbook and starting to read about Le Chatelier's Principle.

Chapter Twenty-One

Jensen

Having someone other than Lily in the passenger seat of my truck feels wrong. Even though Lily's plans changed, Delilah didn't, and she still needed a ride. Lily insisted that I follow through with my promise, and she is following behind in her car. Delilah is charged, fueled by the promise of a recording deal and the end of the year. The difference between her exuberant energy and Lily's calm acceptance is instantly noticeable. Has Delilah always been this exhausting? I chuckle as we pull into the pasture, and Delilah bounces, clapping happily. She hops out of my truck, stretching for the sky like we have been on the road for hours and not the fifteen minutes it takes to hit the countryside.

Grayson immediately starts unloading the instruments, and Delilah heads toward the bonfire. Grayson and I exchange a look before we grab more gear to set up on the half barn. On my second load, I see Delilah talking to Lily, who is sitting on a hay bale. They head toward the keg, and I groan. I was really, really, really hoping to keep Delilah sober tonight so I could spend time with my girl. Now, I may have two drunk girls on my hands.

"If this goes sideways, you're dealing with Delilah," I say to Grayson, and he shoots me the finger.

"*Fat chance. She is mean when she's drunk,*" He signs back. I flip him off in return before I check to make sure the bumpy ride didn't throw my guitar out of tune. Lily brings Delilah a cup and smiles at me across the stage. I'm glad she and Dee are finally starting to get along, but I miss having her all to myself. I tell myself it is better this way, but a part of me wishes it could be just the two of us. I always thought Wild Child Reckless was what I wanted. Now all I seem to want is Lily to myself.

"What's going on, motherfuckers?" Delilah speaks into the mic, and the field of drunk teenagers responds with a raucous "whoo-hoo." Delilah grins. "Hell yeah! Let's get it started! Grab your girl or guy if you haven't already, and let's have fun!"

We launch into our favorite dance set, and I can't help but match Delilah's exuberance as we play a mix of country, rock, and pop. We play for several hours, only stopping for a drink and a wink at Lily, who is dancing off to the side of the stage. The ground around her is empty, as no one is drunk or dumb enough to face my wrath for messing with her. She is more than a few drinks in if her big smile and dance moves are any indication.

We just finished a song when I see Lily gesturing frantically at Delilah. I can't hear what they say, but Lily looks panicked, and that is not okay. Delilah blanches, and I am in the process of putting my guitar down to see what's wrong when Delilah whispers something in Lily's ear that has her tugging on Delilah and shaking her head no. Delilah turns to me, and I recognize that look on her face.

"Fucking hell," I growl as she signs the name of a song that I know will cause nothing but trouble. "Delilah, are you sure? We still need to polish that one. Look, let's just pack up. It's getting late anyway. I'll stop and get us stuffed crust pizza on the way home." I'm practically begging at this point. I don't know what Lily told her, but whatever it was, it isn't good, and I don't want to be here when shit goes down.

"No. C'mon," she signs at us, and I sigh, glancing at Grayson, but I return to my microphone and strum the opening riffs. I see a new truck pull up in the front of a line of new vehicles, and I curse under my breath. People spill out of the trucks, and I grit my teeth. Alexander has a tiny blonde with him. That explains why Delilah wants to do this song now.

Delilah starts dancing along to the song, egging on the crowd. We've never run a completely family-friendly show, but the moves she's pulling now are more suited to the stage and pole than a concert. The more the song goes on, the wilder the crowd gets. Guys are crowding to the stage, and Lily actually gets up on stage, her eyes darting around frantically.

"Did y'all like that?" Delilah calls out as the song ends. Everyone goes crazy. "Well, if you liked that one, I'm sure you'll love this even more! Boys?" She turns and signals for another song, but I must put my foot down.

Grabbing her arm, I pull her back from the mic. "Delilah, no. C'mon. Let's go."

She yanks her arm away and glares at me. "No. We're doing this. C'mon."

I know that look on her face. I fucking hate that look on her face. Tugging her closer, I mutter, "Afterward, we leave. Promise me, Delilah, or I will pack up and drive off without you." I'm so dead serious right now it isn't even funny. Lily was actually scared because of this stupid shit between Delilah and Alexander, and so I am officially over it.

"Fine. Yes. After this, if you want, we can leave. Promise." I meet her eyes, conveying how serious I am about this. Then I turn, catching Lily's hand and reassuring her that we will go after this song. She's shooting Delilah and the crowd worried looks, but she nods at my assurance. Frustrated, I head back to my mic and strike the opening cords.

This song is more provocative than the last, and Delilah uses the poles of the half barn to her advantage. I groan at the number of guys at the foot of the stage. Getting out of here is going to be a bitch. That is the last thing I need. I am one of the only stone-cold sober people in this field besides Grayson, and frankly, I am beginning to resent that fact. There is not enough booze to make this night bearable. Thankfully, the song ends. I turn toward Dee to see Alexander dragging her to the feed room. Fuckin' finally. Maybe now they will get out whatever is between them and they can stop fucking up my life.

"Kennel up," I sign to Grayson, our code for get your shit and yourself in the car so we can get the fuck out of here. I am over this night; it was supposed to be a fun chance to spend time with my girl, but instead, I'm stuck babysitting Delilah.

I barely get half the gear broken down before Delilah bursts out of the feed room, signing an angry kennel up of her own before she grabs Lily and heads for the keg. "Motherfucker," I snarl. We finally load the rest of the kits, and I search for Lily and Delilah. I find them arguing and stride over.

"Dee. You promised. Let's go. Hey." I wave my hands at her, but her eyes are glued to the other side of the bonfire. Glancing over, I see Alexander with the tiny blonde on his lap going to town. I groan, throwing my head back. I must be being punished for something because this weekend couldn't be more of a shit show if we invited the parental units to the party.

"Let's go." Delilah's tone is subdued, and Lily and I look at her nervously. Delilah is always so loud and confident, to hear anything but that is downright scary. She climbs into the front seat of my truck without saying another word. Grayson looks at Lily and me in confusion before climbing into the backseat.

Turning, I kiss Lily. "I'll see you at home, okay? The rest of the weekend is ours. No band, no parents, nothing but just us, okay?" The smile Lily gives me is radiant, and she nods happily. After assuring myself she is okay to drive, I hop into my truck. Now to get rid of my passengers as quickly as possible.

Chapter Twenty-Two

Lily

I grab a bottle of water when Jensen walks in the front door. I can see him visibly relax when he sees me in the kitchen. "Hey, angel baby, I was worried you'd be in bed by the time I got home!"

I chuckle. "No, I was waiting for you. It is kind of late, though." Striding into the kitchen, Jensen grabs a basket from the pantry and starts loading it with premade sandwiches, water, fruit from the fridge, and chips and cookies. "Uh, Jensen. You know something I don't?"

He grins as he shuts the basket. "Oh, angel baby. I know a lot of things you don't know." He brushes a kiss against my lips as he pulls me with him out of the kitchen and back out into the night to his truck.

Once he loads everything into the back seat, he buckles me into the front seat. "There we go. Back where you belong." He kisses me again before joining me in the cab and starting the truck. "So, I got some good and bad news, angel baby. Which do you want first?"

I swallow roughly. I've got good news and bad news is the third worst sentence you can say to someone in the history of the world. "Well, tonight has already been..... interesting..." I can see his jaw harden at my description. I knew he was upset about the night and how Delilah behaved; I wasn't too happy with her either. "Go ahead and give me the bad news first."

Jensen sighed, reaching over and grabbing my hand, twining our fingers together. "Well, you know we signed with the label and will leave after school for L.A. But there is a small chance that we could leave sooner. For now, it is pretty set to be after graduation though."

I can feel the lump forming in my throat. "I thought we would have more time. I knew y'all were negotiating and speaking with people, but I didn't realize it would be so soon." I can feel the tears start to gather in my eyes. "If that's the bad news, then the good news better be pretty fucking spectacular."

Jensen chuckles and kisses my knuckles. "Well, we have the weekend just for the two of us, and I have some pretty big plans. They start tonight."

"Does it have something to do with the picnic basket?" I ask, glancing at the food that won't stay fresh if we don't eat it tonight. Midnight picnics on a Friday aren't typical for us, though Jensen loves taking me on picnics—just never at night. He pulls up to the Winchester house and grins.

"You know it, angel baby. I was going to wait until tomorrow, but after that shitshow of a party, I need some time with you. I miss you."

I smile looking at the dilapidated house. "It must have been beautiful back in the day." The faded white siding is covered in algae, and the shutters are rotten and crooked, but the wrap-around porch has always drawn me in. Jensen and I have explored every inch of this place over the years, and I've told him everything I'd do if I owned it. He always listened, smiling and saying, "Whatever you want, angel baby," even when I went on about a long family table where everyone could celebrate every holiday together.

One afternoon this past summer, I asked him what he'd want if he owned the house. He just looked at me and said, "You. As long as you're here, I have everything I could ever want."

We pull past the house, heading to the pasture and my tree. This has to be one of my favorite places in Havenbrook, and it has become our habit to come here after I have to attend an event for Father. I need the quiet it brings and the security that Jensen represents. If I had to say I had a favorite place in the world, it would be Jensen's arms and this tree. Jensen kills the truck and runs around to pull me down. I love that when we're alone, Jensen touches me every chance he gets. As if reading my mind, he backs me against the truck and kisses me deeply until we are both panting for air. Stepping back reluctantly, he pulls the basket and a blanket from the back seat of his truck.

Spreading the blanket on the ground, he puts the basket down and draws me between his legs.

Soon, the headlights switch off, leaving us with nothing but starlight to see by. The sky is clear, I can see for miles, and I sigh in happiness, leaning back against him. He quickly kisses my temple before passing me a sandwich and a water bottle. We eat in silence, enjoying being next to each other and the peace of a country night. I crumble up my wrapper, tossing it into the basket as Jensen draws out a container of strawberries.

I reach for one, but Jensen taps my hand. "Let me." I sit back against him and let him slowly feed me berry after berry. I nip his fingertips playfully, and he growls. "Careful, angel baby, you're going to start something." I grin in the dark, knowing he can't see my face. When he brings the next berry to my lips, I take a finger instead, running my tongue up and down the digit. I hear the rumble in his chest and know I am playing with fire.

Jensen clears his throat. "I am going to give you one more chance, angel baby. Don't start something you don't want to finish." I know exactly what I am doing. The first time I took him into my mouth, we were in this spot. I thought he was going to pass out, his eyes rolled so far back into his head. Neither of us had any idea what we were doing, but he swears it was perfect and there was no way he could ever have better. Given how quickly he came, I have to conclude I did something right.

Sitting up on my knees, I turn around to face him, and he pulls me tight against his chest. Jensen takes a bite of the berry before rubbing it across my lips, following it with his tongue. I meet his tongue with mine, and we duel for a second before he yanks me onto his lap and kisses me like he may never get to kiss me again. *He may not.* a voice whispers in my mind, and I shove it back down. I refuse to think about that now while I'm here with this man.

Jensen rises to his knees, locking my legs around his waist before lowering me gently to the ground. I run my hands into his hair and tug just how he likes, and he groans in response. His mouth trails down my neck to the hem of my tank top. With his teeth, he pulls it down below my bra, then bites my nipple through the padding. I arch up, grinding myself against him, and he pushes me back into the ground. Unclipping the front clasp of my bra, Jensen's mouth immediately closes around a nipple. At the same time, his hand plucks at the other. "Jensen," I cry out, not even attempting to be quiet. There is no one around to hear me for miles.

Jensen grins up at me before cooing. "What's the matter, angel baby? Do you like that?" That rat, he knows damn good and well that I do. I try to glare at him, but he wraps his lips back around my nipple, scraping it with his teeth, and all thoughts flee my head. Chuckling, he moves to the snap on my jean shorts and pops the button. "Lose the boots, angel baby." I kick them off at such speed I am unsure where they land. As he kisses down my stomach, he tugs my shorts down lower. They have barely reached my knees before he licks my pussy through my panties, nibbling and biting in the way he knows drives me crazy.

I try to open my legs wider, but the shorts trap them. I whine, trying to reach out to shove them down further, when he captures my hands by the wrist, holding them down. "What's the matter, angel baby? Am I teasing you?"

Panting, I try to sit up and glare at him. "You know you are!"

Taking another long lick and nibbling at my pussy, he just stares up at me innocently. "Well then, maybe you shouldn't have teased me all night dancing by the stage for everyone to see." I start to protest, but he hooks my panties and pulls them down and off with my shorts before shoving my legs over his shoulders and sliding his tongue through my slick center.

My back arches of its own accord, and I can't help the sounds pouring from my lips. He scrapes my clit with his tongue, and I come undone, crying out loud, but Jensen doesn't stop there. I can feel a hand slide up my leg until a finger teases my opening, and my breath catches in my throat. We have done a lot together but never anything like this. I can feel his eyes on my face, watching my reaction as he slowly slides the digit into my channel. When I don't protest, he slides it deeper, slowly moving it in and out before adding a second finger to the first. It feels different but amazing at the same time. The stretch is there and burns slightly, but the pleasure of Jensen's tongue on my clit drowns it out.

Jensen laps at my clit, swirling and tapping as his fingers move in and out of me. The more noise I make, the more Jensen increases his pace until I can feel myself shatter over his hand. "That's right, angel baby. Fall apart for me. Just like that."

Jensen's encouragement has me shattering a second time, and when I do, he slides up on top of me, and I notice for the first time that he's naked. "Tell me to stop, Lily." The use of my given name snaps my eyes to him as he settles in between my legs, his hard cock pressed against my entrance. "Tell me to stop, and this ends now. I want to take this step with you, but only if you're fully there with me."

I hold my breath, my eyes searching his, and all I can see is devotion, so I nod. "Yes, Jensen. Please. Yes."

His breath whooshes from his chest, and his cock starts to slide inside me. "I'm so sorry, angel baby; I know this will hurt some. If I could take it, I would, but I can't." His lips are right against my ear as he whispers apologies and praises how good I feel. He's shallowly thrusting inside me, not all the way in, but giving me a chance to get more accustomed to his size.

I appreciate it, but I want more. The last thing I want is for Jensen to treat me like a delicate piece of glass. I take a chance and bite his earlobe before whispering, "Please, Jensen. Fuck me. Now. I need you."

Jensen goes completely still before crashing his lips on mine. I wrap my arms around his neck and kiss him back just as hotly. I am panting and dripping wet when he releases my lips, pulling back and slamming down to the hilt inside of me.

It hurts. My body arches up in protest. I didn't realize it was going to hurt this much. I cry out, and he stops moving immediately, holding himself up by his forearms on top of me, panting and whispering words of encouragement in my ear. I can feel the sting of tears in my eyes, but when Jensen moves to take a nipple back into his mouth, I can feel the pain starting to ease, and my body starts to relax back onto the blanket.

Jensen shifts to look me in the eyes, and I nod. He starts to move again slowly, watching my face for my reaction. Seeing no more pain on my face, his pace increases, and I hold on, hooking my legs around his waist and arching into him, meeting him thrust for thrust. I can feel my orgasm starting to build again, and he slides a finger down to swirl around my clit in rough circles. I scream my pleasure to the sky with the stars as the only witnesses.

Jensen follows behind me, his face buried in the curve of my neck. There are words of praise and assurance on his lips as he fills me up until I can feel it sliding out of me onto the blanket. When the tremors finally stop racking his body, Jensen settles next to me, pulling me into his arms. I cuddle up to his side, my head on his chest and arms around his body, and I fall into the best sleep I have ever known.

Chapter Twenty-Three

Jensen

I wake up to my phone ringing. Lily is still asleep in my arms. The sun rises over the horizon, and I look down at the sleeping woman in my arms. Her hair is tangled into a mess, and I can see my love bites all over her body, and I smile. At some point during the night, Lily ended up wearing my shirt, and I smiled at the sight. When my phone rings again, I pick it up before it wakes Lily.

"Dee, what the hell? Are you okay?" I can hear her tears through the line, and I sit up, but the words that come out of her mouth next have the bottom falling out of my stomach.

"Jensen, Operation No Quitter is a go. I'm hanging up and calling the label. I need you to get in touch with Grayson so we can be on our way as soon as possible. I want to have tickets in my hand this afternoon."

My mouth opens and closes a few times as I look back at the sleeping woman beside me. "Dee, I—"

She cuts me off, and I can hear the tears in her voice. "Jensen. This is not a drill. If you have ever been my friend, I need you now. We have to leave Havenbrook."

I sigh, softening my tone. "Oh, Dee. I'll wake Grayson up. It'll be okay. I promise. Okay?"

I hear a car door open and the key in the ignition. "Thanks, Jenner, you're a savior. I love you. I'll call you when I get an answer about the tickets."

When she clicks off the line, I look at the sleeping woman beside me again. I know there will surely be someone who doesn't think I'm the greatest. I text the service we have set up for Grayson for emergencies. They will ping his TTY phone until he wakes up and then relay the message. Until that happens, I can still pretend I am not about to leave the most important woman in my life the day after I sleep with her for the first time.

I pull her back into my arms and kiss her softly, and Lily smiles against my lips before returning the kiss. Things heat up quickly, and before I know it, Lily is wrapping her perfect lips around my dick. I try to find it in me to protest, but the silkiness of her tongue and the heat of her mouth scrambles what is left of my good intentions. I wrap a hand in her tangled curls and guide her head up and down my length, gritting my teeth so I don't try to force more than she can take.

"Jensen?" Lily looks up at me as her small hand slides up and down my cock. "I want to try something. Is that okay?"

She licks the head as she asks, and at that moment, I would give her anything she wanted if she didn't stop again. "Angel baby, you can do whatever you like to me, within reason." I smirk at her mischievous grin, and she takes my length back into her mouth, causing my head to fall back again. I can feel her wrap her tiny hands around the base of my cock, and then her mouth leaves me.

I open my eyes to say something, only to see her moving to poise herself on top of me before slowly sliding down. "Jesus fucking Christ on a cracker!" I can't help the words as her perfect heat encases me. She's so tight it feels like her pussy is trying to strangle me. Lily moans softly as she settles onto my lap, adjusting to this new position. "Angel baby, if you're too sore—"

I can't finish the sentence before she lifts up and back down again. Biting her bottom lip, she moves until she finds a good rhythm, and I will definitely not complain. I lift my hips to meet her, gripping her thighs. Watching the way her tits bounce as she moves makes me want to give thanks to anyone who will listen about the perfection of the woman on top of me. I close my eyes, moving with her as we race for completion.

I'm also doing anything to quiet that voice in my head reminding me of my promise to Delilah. I have never been this torn in my life. Delilah is my best friend, and I love her and the band, but this woman on top of me stole my heart the moment I first saw her big blue eyes staring at me from over a country bonfire. That was it. I was done. No matter how long I live, there will never be anyone else for me. Hopefully, she forgives me for what is about to happen. Hopefully, she understands.

"Jensen!" she cries out my name, and I lock the sound in my heart to bring out on the days to come without her. I sit up to tug her lips to meet mine. The change in angle tips her over the edge, and the feel of her muscles rippling sends me right behind her. We sit there, still joined, for what feels like an eternity, our labored breaths mingling. I brush my lips against hers and pull her close, knowing without a doubt my next words will destroy the Eden we have here together.

"Angel baby, Delilah called." Lily stills against me, her head resting on my heart. "The timeline has been moved up for L.A."

I swallow roughly when she sits back to look me in the eye. "How soon?" The tears in her eyes gut me.

Sucking in a deep breath, I cup her face. "Today. This afternoon, possibly tomorrow if there are no flights out." Lily gasps, the tears making their way down her face. I swipe them away with my thumbs. "I'm so sorry. I never thought it would be this early, but Delilah is waiting on word from the label, and I had to call the TTY team for Grayson."

Wordlessly, Lily reaches out for her clothes, slips her bra on, and pulls her tank top over her head. "Angel baby," I start to plead with her, but she gets up off me and goes for her shorts, pulling them up her legs. "Please, angel baby, talk to me." I start reaching for my clothes as well.

"What's the point? It's done. You're leaving. I'm going to Wellesley. Maybe it's better this way. A clean break." Lily has gathered the trash from last night and shoved it into the basket.

I'm kicking my boots on when she yanks up the blanket, almost causing me to fall over.

I tear the blanket from her hands and stalk toward her. Her back is against the tree, and she's staring up at me, trembling. I feel bad for a second, then I notice her pupils are dilated. She's not scared; she's turned on. I press her back into the tree trunk, planting both hands on either side of her head. "This is *not* the end. This is *not* over. This is *everything*. *You* are *everything*. I would have thought I made that abundantly clear over the years, but if you need a reminder..."

My lips crash down onto hers; she shoves against my chest for only a second before melting into me. I shove her tank top up around her waist, and she breaks the kiss.

"What about Delilah? You said—"

I interrupt her. "Fuck Delilah. Fuck the band and L.A. and anything that isn't you, angel baby. If it means your happiness, I will burn my world and everyone in it. If you doubt that for even a second, I haven't done my job."

"Jensen." Her whisper is whipped away by the wind that's kicked up as storm clouds roll in. We stand there gazing at each other in silence. Lily must see something in my eyes because she sighs and then smiles sadly. "You've worked too hard and for too long not to go to L.A. now."

I tilt her chin up. "Lily." I use her name so she can tell how serious I am now. "We are not over. I will be back. I will fly you out when I can."

Lily smiles while fixing her tank top and patting my cheek. "Let's go before Delilah starts blowing up your phone." I kiss her softly before picking up the basket and blanket and loading them into the back seat of my truck. Lily is already settled in the passenger seat when I shut the back door, and I shoot her a look, showing my displeasure. Lily grins and sticks her tongue out at me.

I turn the truck around just as the rain starts to fall. Lily turns and watches as our tree gets further away. We pass the Winchester house and hit the main road. I take Lily's hand in mine as she settles back into the seat. "Let's make a promise. Every Christmas, no matter what, we meet back at our spot."

Lily turns and stares at me. "Will you be able to? What about touring and your concerts?"

I shrug. "I'm not sure what we will be doing at first, and if the label doesn't like it, I don't really care. Every Christmas. Promise?"

Lily nods her head. "Every Christmas. Promise."

Chapter Twenty-Four

Lily

I sit beside Jensen, doing my best to hide the fact that my heart is breaking. For once, the skills I learned living with Father come in handy. Jensen gets a text from Grayson on the way, so we swing by to pick him up before heading to Delilah's house. When we pull into the driveway, no other vehicles are in sight. Jensen heads up to the door, but Delilah pulls up beside us in her mother's truck before he reaches it. One look at her face, and Jensen pulls her into his arms. Grayson and I get out of the truck and hang back. I notice when Delilah spots me—her eyebrows shoot up to her hairline. While I've been here a few times before, I usually stay at the house when Jensen comes here for practice.

"Lillian's gonna take us to the airport and drive my truck home. I didn't want to leave it in long-term parking until Dad could finally pick it up," Jensen tells her, and I keep my face neutral, but hearing my full name from Jensen stings. He mouths "sorry" back at me before following Delilah into the house. She is discussing travel plans and things the label has promised, and I sit on the couch and wait. When she says she wants to record one more song, I frown. I thought leaving was so crucial that it couldn't wait. If she has time to record a song, I could have had more time with Jensen.

We all follow her back into their makeshift studio. Once again, I am awed by the very expensive-looking equipment. Jensen sets some of it up while I browse the pictures pinned to the wall. There are shots of the group, but several with just Jensen and Delilah. I look closer at one that appears to be from a pool party. Delilah's bright red curls are piled high on her head, and her emerald-green bikini makes her eyes shine even brighter. Jensen is cuddled up next to her, making faces at the camera.

I glance over as Delilah starts singing and playing her guitar for the camera. Jensen follows along, and Grayson adds a mellow beat. The song is so melancholy that it makes me want to cry. I briefly watch them, then focus on the pictures on the wall. Jensen and I will never have this—public and happy. We'll always be hidden in the shadows. I swallow hard as tears threaten. It isn't supposed to end like this. It isn't fair. I'm supposed to have more time. I quickly wipe my eyes and smile when Jensen looks back at me. He frowns but is quickly distracted by Delilah.

I take the chance to slip out and crank the truck. It's bigger than my car, but I can manage. It's a straight shot to the airport. The drive is quiet. Delilah is on her phone, and Jensen stares at me like he's trying to memorize every detail. I keep my eyes on the road, refusing to look at him. I knew this would hurt when I learned they were moving to L.A. The airport is packed, and I have to circle the parking lot a few times before we find the drop-off spot. Grayson grins and points out the sign we somehow missed. I pull under the awning, and Delilah and Grayson grab their bags.

Jensen cups my cheek, and I lean into his touch. "Angel baby, I—" He stops as Delilah opens the door.

"C'mon, we've got to check-in. Thanks for the ride, Lillian!"

Jensen hesitates and then follows Delilah out of the truck. My grip tightens on the steering wheel, knuckles white.

"I want a text when you're home safe, okay?" Jensen says, his hazel eyes warm with concern.

"Of course. I'll text when I get home, and you let me know when you land?"

"If you weren't driving, I'd text as soon as you left, but focus on the road. Be safe for me, Angel Baby." Jensen shuts the door, letting Delilah lead him inside. I merge back into traffic, feeling the ache in my chest grow. The further I go, the worse it gets until a sob finally breaks free. I pull into a McDonald's parking lot and let my heart shatter.

I'm so tired. I'm tired of pretending. I am tired of waiting for the other shoe to drop. I'm tired of my life never being my own. I slam my hands against the steering wheel, the pain clearing my head a little. I do it again. And again. Rain begins to pour, and I sit there as the sky weeps. It could have been minutes, it could have been hours, but I finally cry myself out. I grab some napkins from the glove compartment to clean my face before returning to the road. I drive home silently, the only sound being the rain pelting the truck.

When I pull up at home, I stare at the house. Mom and Mike aren't home yet, so I head inside and go straight to Jensen's room. The smell of his spicy cologne still lingers in the air. I take a deep breath and hold it in my lungs. I steal his blanket and pillow off his bed and return to my room.

I wake up to my text alert. I snatch my phone off my side table, thinking it will be Jensen, but I see a text from my father's secretary, Ms. Lassiter. She's trying to schedule my move back to the governor's mansion. What? When I question the move, I get a message stating that my father requires me over the summer. I will transition to my college apartment the week before the semester starts. Sighing, I lay back on the pillow, staring at the ceiling. I double-check that Jensen has yet to text, but my screen remains blank. I pull his blanket up again and try to go back to sleep. When that doesn't happen, I go to the kitchen. Some hot cocoa may help. I'm making some when Mom wanders into the kitchen in her robe.

"There you are Lily-Bean. You were sound asleep when we got home. You feeling okay?" I shrug a shoulder and go back to fixing my drink. "Look. I know your time here was short, but you know you're welcome anytime, right? There is always a room here for you. This will always be your home." She thinks I'm upset I'm moving back with Father, which is not entirely wrong.

"Thanks, Mom." I smile at her as I stir the chocolate mix into my warmed milk. "I appreciate that. I got the text from Ms. Lassiter earlier. They already want to start getting things ready to move. I know I have no choice if I get to stay or go, but I would like to return for Christmas. Is that okay?"

I'm enveloped in a tight hug. "Oh, honey, of course! You are welcome here whenever you want, just say the word. I may not be as powerful or have as much as your father, but I will always do whatever I can to ensure your happiness, Lily-Bean. Never ever doubt that." She cups my cheeks in her hands, her eyes boring into mine.

"Thanks, Mom," I whisper before returning to my room. Sitting at my desk, I recheck my phone. Nothing. I open the messaging app before closing it again. No. I'm not going to do it. I'm not going to be the one to text first. I'm not. Instead, I open up VidReel. There has been no new activity on Wild Child Reckless or Jensen's page. I stare at the painting on my wall, and the memories of the last three years flicker through my mind like a cartoon drawing.

I stare back at the dark phone screen. I pick up my phone and plug it into the charger before sitting it on my bedside table. They say that silence is also an answer, and Jensen's silence speaks volumes. I'm not silly enough to think he would be glued to his phone texting me, but I at least deserved a text letting me know he landed. Absence shows where your heart truly stands—and where you really stand in theirs. I tug Jensen's blanket over my head and cry myself to sleep surrounded by his scent.

Chapter Twenty-Five

Jensen

Being in L.A. is overwhelming. You think you're prepared, but you just wander around like a fool when it happens. Delilah still won't tell me why we left Havenbrook so suddenly. Between seeing where we'll stay, meeting with the label, and being told to find a pianist, I'm ready to throw in the towel when I get back to my room. I spot my phone charging on the side table and curse. The day was so hectic I forgot to text Lily. I pick up my phone, expecting a flood of messages, but there's only one—from Dad, asking how the first day went. I check the time, mentally adding two hours for the time difference; it's nearly ten p.m. back home. I feel like an ass. The thought of Lily going to bed without even a good night from me twists my insides.

Lying in bed, staring at the L.A. skyline, I grab my phone and text Lily.

Sorry I missed getting back to you. Things were crazy when we landed. I hope you made it home safely and are sleeping well. I miss you more than you can ever know.

I stare at the screen, waiting for a reply. Sighing, I respond to my dad, and we chat briefly about what's next. I wish him goodnight and get ready for bed. I'm leaving the bathroom when there's a knock on my door.

"Come in!" Delilah walks in, dressed in sweats and a ragged gray tee from the football team. Her red nose stands out against her pale skin. "Dee?" She sniffles, and I immediately pull her into my arms. She starts to sob, so I guide her to the bed and hold her close. "Dee, what's going on?" Dee shakes her head, burying her face in my chest. I give up trying to get answers and settle us against the pillows.

I flip on the T.V. and scroll through the channels, landing on a late-night showing of *Twister*. Growing up in the South, I've been through my fair share of tornado seasons, but the weather still fascinates me. I glance down halfway through the movie to find Dee sound asleep, pressed against my side. I sigh. *Fuck.* Moving her without waking her is impossible, and that's the last thing I want to do. Reaching over her, I check my phone. Still no text. Lily must be asleep, or she's mad that I didn't text and is ignoring me.

Call me when you wake up, angel baby. I miss your voice. Good night.

I put the phone back on the bedside table and settle down to sleep. It doesn't take long before I'm out like a light.

The ringing of a phone wakes me. I roll over, forcing my eyes open and reaching for it, but it stops abruptly. I hear a female voice answer.

"Hello? Oh hey, Lillian. No, I think he's still asleep. Let me check." Dee pokes me on the shoulder. "Hey, are you awake? Lillian is on the phone." I close my eyes, praying this is just a bad dream—that Dee didn't answer my phone and Lily isn't on the other end. I pray harder than ever, wishing I could be spared this. At this moment, I'd rather be put out of my misery than take this call.

"Jensen!" Delilah snaps, and I open my eyes to see her holding out the phone. I take it reluctantly. "I wonder if they have coffee in this place," Dee muses aloud as she heads for the kitchen. I wait for the door to click shut then lift the phone to my ear.

"Good morning, angel baby." My heart races, but I try to keep my voice calm.

"Why was Delilah answering your phone at six a.m.?" The sadness in her voice twists my stomach. I clear my throat. Nothing has ever happened between Dee and me. I might've entertained that idea when I was younger, but it was always a pipe dream. Delilah and I would never work. Realizing I've been silent too long, I clear my throat again.

"It's not what you think, angel baby. Dee came into my room last night crying, and I couldn't move her without waking her up. She must've forgotten where she was and answered my phone." I hear Lily gasp on the other end.

"She spent the night with you? In your bed?" The hurt in her voice feels like a punch to the gut.

"Angel baby, it wasn't like that. I promise. You know you're it for me." I've spent the last three years trying to prove this to her, and one night may have undone it all. I should've just moved Dee—who cares if she woke up.

"I fucked up. I'm sorry." I can't live with myself if I have messed this up already. I've barely been gone twenty-four hours.

"It's okay." Lily's voice is so quiet I can barely hear her. "I'm going to go. I have to get ready for school and start packing."

"Packing?" My heart starts to race. Why is she packing?!

Lily sighs. "Yes, Jensen. I'm packing. I am moving back in with Father over the summer before I move to my apartment in Boston. I got the text yesterday. I was going to tell you sooner, but...." But she never heard from me. The rest of the sentence hangs in the air.

"Why would you go back to Austin? Why not just stay in Havenbrook until college starts?"

"I don't have a choice Jensen. Father told me that I am coming back and to be ready, so I am going back," Lily's voice snaps, causing me to raise my eyebrows. Lily has never been one to anger this quickly. Then again, she has never called me when I was in bed with another woman—platonically or otherwise.

"Okay. Okay." I keep my tone as calm as possible. "I'm sorry. I'll do better about keeping in touch. Yesterday was just a bit much, and I forgot. I'm sorry." I realize I sound like a broken record, but from 1500 miles away, my choices are limited. Lily sighs.

"It's fine, Jensen. I know you're going to be busy now. I still have to finish finals and classes while packing and returning to Austin. Let's play it by ear. We can see how it goes." I'm not too fond of this—at all.

"I don't like this." I can't let her think I am okay with not having her in my life every day. I can't imagine not hearing her voice or seeing her face.

Lily laughs softly. "You may not like it, Jensen, but it is the best option."

I growl. "You're damn right I don't like it. You are more important than anything I have going on here. We both know I will be busy, but I promise you will get at least a good morning and good night text from me, and I want a phone call every Sunday morning."

Lily chuckles, "Yeah. Okay, Jensen, you got it." I can hear the sarcasm dripping from her tone, and it makes me more determined to keep our schedule.

"And don't forget Christmas. Our spot. You and me. Now, go ahead and get ready to head to class. I have to prepare and see what the label wants to do about this pianist they want us to hire. It's going to be almost impossible."

Lily chuckles weakly before whispering goodbye and hanging up.

I chuck my phone onto the bed. Fucking hell. I hear the door creak as Dee pushes it open, holding two steaming cups of coffee. I glare at her from the bed, and she pulls up short. "Whoa. What did I do?"

"Why did you answer my phone?" Dee looks shocked at my aggressive tone.

"I was asleep. It was ringing. It was a habit. I didn't even think about it. Why? Since when can I not answer your phone?"

I groan, not ready to explain exactly why my best friend can't answer the phone when my stepsister calls. "Forget it. Is one of those mine?"

Dee sits a cup on the bedside table before stepping back.

"No. I was gonna double fist the cups today. Of course one is yours. Jensen, why can't—" God must have been making up for earlier because, at that moment, Grayson comes to the door with his cup of coffee in hand.

"Cora wants us to go through these headshots and pick at least ten candidates to audition, and I am not doing this alone. Get your asses out here." Grayson looks at each of us before returning to the living room.

"Just forget it, Dee." I pick up my coffee cup and head to the living room. "We have bigger problems to solve." Let the hunt begin.

Chapter Twenty- Six

Lily

Jensen has been in L.A. for three weeks. Since that first night, he has kept his word. I get good morning and good night texts every day, and he calls every Sunday morning. They are no closer to finding a pianist than when they arrived. Everyone is getting frustrated. Graduation is over. Everything is packed up from my room in Mom's house except the furniture. I stand in the room, think back on the memories, and my eyes land on my painting. Mom will ship it to me when I get to Boston. I don't want to risk Father getting rid of it.

Closing my bedroom door, I walk down the hallway and see Mom and Mike waiting for me in the foyer.

"We're gonna miss you, kiddo. Knock them dead in Boston." Mike's hug is warm and genuine, and I can feel myself tearing up.

"I'm going to miss you too. Don't forget. Mail me some of Abuela's pan de polvo as soon as you can."

He chuckles before shooting finger guns at me. "You got it, sweetheart. You drive safe."

Mom wraps me in her arms, and I stand there breathing in her scent while she strokes my hair. "I'm going to miss you, Lily-bean." I can hear the sadness in her voice, so I hug her tighter.

"I'm going to miss you, Mom. I'll be back at Christmas though. I've already cleared it with Father." That had been surprisingly easy. I'm still waiting for the other shoe to drop.

Mom sniffles, wiping at the tears beneath her eyes. "Yes, you will. I am counting down the days." She hugs me one more time. I grab my keys from the entrance table one last time. I head outside in the heat, hitting the remote start on my car. Settling into the driver's seat, I look back at the house and see Mom and Mike waving from the porch. I wave back before putting the car in reverse and pulling out of the drive. I make it to the corner before the tears start to fall. My heart is breaking all over again. I don't want to leave and return to the frozen hell I was in before. I want warmth and laughter and love. Everything that makes the Parker house a home. A tear lands on my knee, another following quickly. I have yet to leave Havenbrook, but I already want to go back home.

Summer is halfway over, and I cannot wait until I am in Boston. At least then, several thousand miles will separate my father from me. Vincent and Marco have been to dinner almost every night, and I have been playing nice, but it is getting on my nerves. I know better than to let my displeasure show on my face, but even I can't take much more. I am looking through my course catalog when a maid knocks on my door and brings in a large vase of red roses. Setting them on my desk, she leaves the room as silently as she entered. Plucking the card from the crimson petals, I open the tiny envelope.

Just something to brighten your day like you do mine. Marco

Rolling my eyes, I toss the card on the desk. Marco has become more and more persistent as the weeks have gone on. I haven't mentioned anything to Jensen about it, but, in my defense, the conversations with Jensen are getting shorter and shorter. I know it isn't his fault. He's just being pulled in so many directions. Last weekend, he even fell asleep on the phone with me while we were talking about the classes I was considering taking. I just hung up the phone and filled out the course sheet myself.

"Who sent those?" I see Clarissa standing in my doorway, staring at the bouquet. I hand the card over before getting a bottle of water from the mini-fridge. "Why on earth would a man as talented and important as Marco be interested in a nobody like you?" Despite her offensive tone, I have to laugh.

"I don't know Clarissa. Why don't you ask him the next time he's over with Vincent?" From the look on her face, I fear she just might. I make a mental note to suddenly have a migraine the next time the Russos are over for dinner. "Did you need something?" Rolling her eyes and harumphing, Clarissa glares at me.

"Your father wanted me to take you shopping for your apartment. He thinks it will be a good idea if we bond, and he wants to ensure your apartment is decorated tastefully." She sneers at my bedroom, which is still reminiscent of how it was when Mom and Father were married, before things changed.

"How about this? You can decorate my apartment however *you* want, with these exceptions," I hold out a handwritten list for her, "and I'll tell Father we picked everything out together and had a wonderful time. Sound good?" Clarissa yanks the list out of my hand and studies it.

"Perfect. I can work with this." She waves the list in the air before leaving the room. I shake my head. The only things on that list were the type of towels I prefer and the fact that I won't sleep in anything smaller than a queen-size bed. Frankly, I couldn't give a rat's ass what is in my apartment. I plan to be focused on my studies. Just because Father bought my admission doesn't mean I don't plan on earning my grades.

My phone beeps with a text notification, and I look down. Jensen!

Hey, angel baby. I'm checking in. How are you? I miss your pretty face. We found a pianist in a speakeasy bar near the record label. She's coming in to audition today. What's new with you?

Speakeasy bar? That's cool. There's nothing new with me. Clarissa came in and wanted to go shopping for my apartment—per my father's edict. I told her to do it, and I would lie and say we went.

That woman needs her head examined, I swear. When do you leave for your apartment?

In three weeks. Father is giving me three weeks to adjust to the area and my schedule before class starts. He threatened to go to Boston to help me get settled. Hopefully, some natural disaster in Texas will keep him in the state. Just kidding. Kinda.

Jensen responds with a string of laughing emoji. Smiling down at my phone, I miss the sound of footsteps outside my room.

"Ah. I see you did receive my flowers. I was wondering when I didn't hear from you." My head snaps up to see Marco Russo standing in my doorway. I shove my phone into my pocket quickly. "I was hoping you would text me when they arrived so I would know." Marco leans casually against the door.

"Marco, what are you doing here?" I move back toward my desk, putting the chair between us as Marco walks further into my room.

"Come now. That's not the way to greet someone who sent you flowers, but I will answer your question this time. I am here with my father. He had an unscheduled meeting with the governor today. I thought I would come along and see if you had received my gift. Do you like them?" Marco is entirely in my bedroom, and his leather shoes are making no sound against the thick rugs on the floor.

"Oh. Yes. They're lovely. Thank you." Marco smiles, placated. He fingers the petals of one of the blooms before sniffing the flower.

"They were quite expensive, but only the best for *moya devushka.*" I hear Vincent call out, and Marco reaches for my hand, dropping a kiss on its back. "Unfortunately, I have to go. I will see you Friday night, *moya krasavitsa.*" He drops my hand and strolls out the door. When I am sure he is gone, I wipe the back of my hand off on my jeans in disgust.

A knock on my door makes me jump. Adrian stands in the doorway, wearing his typical scowl of disapproval. "Your father wants to see you." I roll my eyes before heading down the hall to my father's study.

"Do you ever tire of being my father's lapdog, Adrian?" The only response is silence and the sound of our shoes against the hardwood floors. As we get to the double doors, I shrug and shove them open. I'm beyond caring about my father's mood today.

"Lillian, finally. You took your time. I just met with Vincent, and as luck would have it, Marco is available to accompany you to Boston to settle into your apartment. You leave in three weeks." I stand across the desk from him, trying to stay calm, but if I didn't know better, I would swear I was having a heart attack. I stumble and sit down in one of the chairs without an invitation, but my knees won't hold me any longer.

"What do you mean Marco is accompanying me to Boston?"

Father huffs in annoyance, looking up from the papers in his hand. "He will be flying with you to Boston and helping you get set up in your apartment, then he will show you around the area. He's going to be up there doing an apprenticeship. I was sure he told you."

I clear my throat a couple of times before finally speaking. "Yes. I believe he mentioned it, but I thought you would take me?"

The sheaf of papers hits the desk, and I can feel his annoyance radiating off him in waves. "Lillian, I am a very busy man. I know you think this office runs itself, but I have many constraints on my time. I just can't get away." I remember my text to Jensen and think of the irony. I would do anything to have Father go to Boston instead of Marco.

"Of course, Father. Thank you. May I be excused?" He waves me off, and I head back to my room. Once I ensure my door is locked, I collapse on my bed and stare at the ceiling. What is my life right now? The phrase be careful what you wish for plays on a loop in my head.

Chapter Twenty-Seven

Jensen

Meeting Mia in that bar feels like a stroke of luck, but Delilah catching Gio Santoro's eye is game-changing. I've always said no man except Alexander could catch Delilah's attention, but seeing her with Gio, I realize I might be wrong. He treats her like a princess, using his industry knowledge and popularity to catapult Delilah and Wild Child Reckless into the spotlight.

In the first few weeks, Delilah works herself to the point of exhaustion, but with Gio in the picture, she's smiling again, returning to her old self. I had my doubts initially, but Gio is all right. I glance at my phone—my next problem. Something's wrong with my angel baby, but she won't say what. The last time we talked, I told her about Gio, how we negotiated a contract, and that the tour was coming soon. She made all the right comments and asked the right questions, but it felt like she wasn't fully present.

When the tour dates are finalized, I call Lily to share the good news, but it goes straight to voicemail. I shrug and go back to packing my bag. It's a five-hour drive to Las Vegas from L.A. I try Lily again, but there is still no answer. Frustrated, I leave a message asking her to call me back. By Monday afternoon, we're in Denver, Colorado, and I try again, with no response. This time, my message isn't as nice. Lily has never ignored my calls.

A thought hits me, and I immediately call my dad.

"Hey, bud, you okay? How's the trip?" Dad sounds relaxed, which is reassuring.

"Hey, Dad, it's going good. Is Gwen around?" If something is wrong with Lily, Gwen will be with her, right?

"Well yeah, son. She's right here. Did you need to talk to her?" Dad's confusion mirrors my own—so why isn't Lily answering?

"I just couldn't get in touch with Lily, so I was making sure everything's okay."

Dad chuckles. "You forgot."

"What do you mean I forgot?" I don't forget things, especially when it comes to Lily.

"She's moving into her apartment in Boston. School starts soon." Oh crap, I did forget. Wrapped up in my own life, I didn't even think to ask about hers. I feel like an idiot.

"I didn't realize it was happening so soon. I thought it was in a few weeks."

"You've been busy with the band and prepping for the tour. Just text her congratulations, and it'll be fine." Dad laughs. "Did you need anything else?"

"No, Dad. Thanks. I'll text you when we hit Detroit."

I hang up and sit there staring at the road for a few minutes. Finally, I scroll through my messages with Lily and don't like what I see. I've barely asked her about her life lately and constantly shifted the conversation back to myself. I'm a jerk. No wonder she's not answering—she's in the middle of a huge move and doesn't have time to listen to me go on about my life. I wouldn't want to talk to me either.

"Hey, angel baby. Good luck with the move. I'd love to hear all about it when you get settled. Let me know if you made it, okay? I miss you."

I set my phone down and pick up my guitar, strumming random chords until they form a rough song. I open the Notion app and hit record; the app's ability to convert live recordings into sheet music has been a lifesaver on the road. I jot down the basic chords and transitions, then put my guitar away. Most of the others have gone to their bunks—Grayson and I agreed to let Delilah and Mia have the private rooms, and we took the bunks in the central area. It makes sense for them to have some privacy.

I grab a water bottle and head to my bunk, spotting my favorite hoodie by the pillow. It's not my favorite because it's the best hoodie—it's Lily's favorite. She always borrowed it when she got chilled, and it still smells like her. I close the bunk curtain and let the bus rocking lull me to sleep.

***

The next thing I know, it's morning. I hear Delilah and Mia chatting, and the smells of coffee and bacon hit me. I drag myself to the main area and plop down at the counter, resting my head in my hands. Delilah slides a coffee cup over, and I take a grateful sip. I pull my phone off the charger, but there's no text waiting for me. I get it—moving is hard, and she probably hasn't had a chance to check her phone.

"We're stopping for fuel, so stretch your legs if you want," the driver announces over the intercom. "We're a little over halfway to Detroit; this might be our last stop for several hours."

I step off the bus into the bright sunlight, squinting as I sip coffee. We're just off the freeway, and commuters are already bustling around. I watch a man exit his car, his phone on speaker, while two kids battle to be heard in the backseat. He just smiles at them. I wonder what it would be like to be that normal, to come home to a family every day. I let the thought wash over me for a moment, imagining how different life could have been.

When we hit the road again, I'm more determined than ever to get Lily on the phone. I text her to warn her that I am about to call her in thirty minutes and not answering is not an option. I add that if I don't hear from her, I will try to contact her father to make sure she is okay.

"Jensen, I can't talk right now. I am dealing with the school and movers moving the last of the furniture. I will text you this evening when I can talk. Please don't bother my father."

I feel bad about forcing an answer from her, but at least I know she is okay. That's the most important thing. I go back to my

Notion app and replay last night's file. Grabbing my guitar, I start to build on the melody, making adjustments. I am on my third playthrough when Delilah sits beside me with her guitar on her lap.

"That's lovely, Jensen!" she hums as she strums the counter-melody. I turn the app back on record, and we repeat the song. Mia walks up with her violin and a kitchen chair. She picks up her bow and effortlessly adds to the song we are building. Grayson has his eyes closed, concentrating on the vibrations from our instruments, breaking them apart from road noise, and begins a rolling beat.

Delilah's eye loses focus, and I watch. I don't think anyone else has seen this, but I know what will happen. When the refrain stops again, she starts to sing.

"What if we were meant to be?
What if we needed to leave
Just to see
That we were too young
We both had growing up to do
Wherever you are
That's where my heart is
Memories float through my dreams
Like a movie scene
What if we were meant to be
What if we messed it up
And gave up too soon?

We loved each other once upon a time
Why not twice?

I check the recording to ensure we got it all down and grin. "Way to go, Dee. That was amazing!" Grayson reads over the lyrics, gives them to Delilah, and then sends the file to himself. I know that he will have the percussion written out before the day is done. I go back to watching the road as Mia tries to teach Delilah the violin. They're laughing and joking, and I have to smile. Everything is falling into place. I look down at my still-blank phone and sigh. Almost everything.

****

We arrive in Detroit and are almost immediately swept into the venue to start sound check. Walking into the empty venue for practice feels like stepping into another world that's quiet, vast, and everything I had ever dreamed of. The house lights are dim, and the only sounds are the echoes of our footsteps and the faint buzz of amps warming up. It's hard to believe that in a few hours, this place will be packed with people, but right now, it's just us, our instruments, and an almost holy silence.

As I climb onto the stage, my nerves kick in, not because of the crowd that isn't here yet but because of what this space represents. It's the calm before the storm, where dreams become reality. My guitar case feels heavier than usual, so I swap hands and set it on the stage. The stage is littered with cables, mic stands, and setlists hastily scribbled on crumpled sheets of paper. It's messy and imperfect, just like us.

I plug in my bass, the familiar crackle of the amp sparking to life. The first strum echoes around the empty hall, bouncing off rows of vacant seats and back to me, magnified and raw. It's just practice, but my heart still skips a beat as I hear the sound fill the space. I glance at the rest of the band, each lost in their world of tuning, adjusting, and mentally preparing. We all share the same nervous energy that buzzes beneath the surface, pushing us forward. Do more. Be more. Live more.

We run through the first song, and it's rough, a little off in places, but that's what this time is for. There's no pressure to be perfect; there is just the need to feel out the space and get comfortable with how the music sounds in a big room. The acoustics are different, the feedback sharper, and every missed note feels magnified, hanging in the air longer than it should.

I take a moment to look back and imagine the seats filled, the crowd's roar replacing the empty echoes. Knowing this quiet, almost sacred space will soon be alive with energy, sound, and light is surreal. I let the thought push me, driving my fingers harder against the strings as we dive into the next song.

This is where we fine-tune, find our rhythm, and get every beat ingrained in muscle memory. This is where dreams become reality. This is where Wild Child Reckless becomes the band it was supposed to be. The band we dreamed of as we played farmers' markets and trade shows. Graduations and birthday parties. This may be practice, but it feels like something more—like the final puzzle piece sliding into place, each chord pulling us closer to that moment when it'll all come alive.

Chapter Twenty- Eight

Lily

Boston feels like a whole new world—alive with the hum of old brick buildings, modern shops, and the salty harbor breeze. Marco navigates the crowd effortlessly while I try to keep up. We end up at La Bella Vita, a cozy café in Beacon Hill, where the air smells of fresh bread, garlic, and something sweet. The menu is full of New England classics. Marco orders like he's a regular, suggesting clam chowder, lobster rolls, and fresh salads. When the food arrives, I realize how hungry I am. The lobster roll is loaded with claw meat in a buttery bun. Marco talks between bites, pointing out landmarks and sharing stories, sounding genuine for once.

We finish with Boston cream pie—a decadent, must-try dessert. Marco pays, and we step outside. "Shall we get your books? Classes start in three weeks, right?" I'm surprised he knows—Jensen didn't even remember I was moving this weekend. Mom mentioned how he called his dad, frantic because I hadn't texted back.

Marco's driver takes us to the campus bookstore. A student assistant gives me a basket and pulls my textbooks while I browse for stationery and testing supplies. As I look at legal pads, Marco approaches with a small leatherbound poetry book. "You like poetry?" I ask.

"My mama used to read it to me. In Russia, the government controls what literature is available, especially in poorer regions. My best memories are of her reading to me by the fire." Marco turns the book over in his hands, lost in thought.

I place my hand on his. "You should get it."

Marco swipes his card at checkout, ignoring my protests and attempts to pay for my own purchases. "Let me do this for you." I thank him, taking the smaller bag while he carries the books. "Do you need anything else? I have a meeting soon, but I can leave my driver if you need to go anywhere."

"No, I'm good. I'll finish unpacking and maybe order pizza."

We pass through Boston's vibrant streets, and Marco teases, "Tell me you don't like pineapple on your pizza."

"I do not," I laugh. "But BBQ chicken pizza? That's my thing. Mike used to make garlic knots that were soft, cheesy, and amazing." My mouth waters at the memory.

"Mike—he married your mama?"

"Yeah, he's Jensen's dad." I recheck my phone—still nothing from Jensen.

Marco's tone softens. "Was he nice to you?"

"The best. He made my favorite desserts and caldo de pollo when I was sick. He always took care of me."

"Good." Marco's voice is firm. We pull up to my building, and he carries the bags to my door. "It wouldn't have gone well for him if he hadn't." His seriousness kills my laughter.

"He's amazing. I miss them all." Marco seems satisfied, smiling at me as he returns to the car. I step inside, placing my keys in the bowl by the door, just like at home.

I close and lock the door before wandering into the kitchen to get a Diet Coke. My phone chimes again and again, and I unlock it to see my Google notifications for the band going off like crazy. They're opening for Gio Santorro tonight. Of course, I knew that was going to be happening soon. I just didn't realize it was this soon. Sitting on the incredibly uncomfortable excuse for a couch, I text Jensen.

Just got back home. Knock them dead tonight. I know you're going to be amazing. Call me after?

Jensen immediately responds with a picture of the band on the stage at what must have been sound check.

I love the picture but get no other response. I shrug my shoulders. Overall, I had a good day, and I know he is busy. He will message me when he has time. If nothing else, he will know I want to hear from him after. I putter around my apartment, folding towels, putting away silverware, and doing all the small things I assured the house manager she didn't have to do. Sighing, I flop back onto my bed and flip on the TV. Usually, I don't particularly appreciate having a TV in my bedroom. But when I saw how bad the couch was, I had the movers bring it in here.

Several hours later, I'm watching a *Supernatural* rerun when I hear the buzzer for the door going off. Shocked, I get up and check my phone. No messages. Who is at my door? I grab my umbrella from the holder and hold it in front of me like a weapon.

"Hello?" I click the speak button, and my grip tightens.

"Heya, I've got a pizza delivery here for Lily DuPont." The guy sounds bored and in a hurry.

"I didn't order any pizza."

"Yeah, the order says it was placed by Marco. Is that your boyfriend? C'mon, lady, do you want the pie or not? I have other deliveries to make." I hit the button to unlock the door, and in minutes, a knock sounds. I remove the chain and open the door to see a younger guy in a pizza delivery uniform.

"No charge. It's been paid. Have a nice night, lady." He thrusts the box into my hand and is gone before I can respond. I lock the door again and reattach the chain before heading into the kitchen. I sit the box on the bar and flip the lid open. It's a BBQ chicken pizza with extra cheese.

"What in the world?" I feel the tears welling up. It has been a while since someone has done something so nice for me, and I'm not sure how to react. My text alert chimes, and I check my phone. It's Marco.

Bon appètit. Let me know how the pizza is. I've never eaten at this place, but it was the closest for delivery. Have a good night.

I grab a few slices, sit in my breakfast nook, and look out over the city as the sun sets. Havenbrook would be rolling up the sidewalks right now—teens would be sneaking out to the pastures for bonfires, beers, and beats. I spent most weekends of the last three years in the same pastures. Sitting here in central Boston, eating pizza delivery, almost boggles my mind. I grab sparkling water from the fridge, store the leftover pizza, and head to my en suite.

Having my own bathroom is a luxury I didn't know I missed after sharing a Jack and Jill with Jensen for so long. The tub is deep and jetted—exactly where I'm heading first. I turn the water as hot as it goes and rummage through the cabinets, appreciating my father's staff for handling little things like stocking bath salts and sparkling water.

"Ah ha!" I find a bottle of lavender bath salts and sprinkle a generous amount. I pin my curls into a messy bun, toss my clothes in the hamper, and step into the steaming water, sinking to my shoulders with a contented sigh. I didn't move boxes today, but my muscles still appreciate this. I fiddle with the buttons until the jets kick on, frothing the water. I could easily fall asleep here, but after an hour, the water cools, and I reluctantly drag myself through the rest of my nighttime routine. By the time my head hits the pillow, I am out like a light—sleeping so soundly that I don't hear my phone as it vibrates across the bathroom counter, forgotten.

Chapter Twenty-Nine

Jensen

Walking out onto the stage feels like stepping into a dream—surreal and electrifying all at once. The lights hit my eyes, blinding me for a second, and all I can do is listen to the crowd. My heart pounds, each beat in sync with the low hum of the crowd, and my senses are on high alert. The air is thick with anticipation, as if every breath I take is charged with electricity.

The first few steps feel heavy, and my legs are almost robotic as I cross the stage. I can hear the faint rustling of the curtains behind me, the thump of my boots on the wooden floor, and the muffled chatter of the audience turning into a low, expectant roar. My guitar strap digs into my shoulder, grounding me in the moment and reminding me that this is real.

The stage smells like stale beer, sweat, and the lingering ozone of amps and cables, a potent mix that already feels like home. I glance at my bandmates—they look as wired as I am, a mix of nerves and adrenaline painted across their faces. We exchange brief, wordless nods that say *we've got this.*

My fingers hover over the strings, tingling with excitement and fear. I grip the neck of my guitar tighter, feeling the familiar, worn wood beneath my hand, and suddenly, the crowd's noise fades into the background. It's just us, ready to pour everything out in a blaze of music and raw energy.

I manage one last deep breath, and the spotlight snaps on, bathing us in its searing heat. This is it—our first performance as an opening act. The first note is like ripping off a Band-Aid—then there's no going back. I let the music take over, feeling the rhythm pulse through my veins. The crowd's energy hits me like a wave, and suddenly, I'm not nervous anymore. I'm alive, and there's no place I'd rather be.

An hour later, we head off the stage to our green room. Maddie ensured there is something here for everyone, including snacks and drinks. Grayson goes high, and I slap his hands with mine before he returns the favor.

"That was *amazing*!!!!" Grayson signs, and he is not wrong. I grab a water bottle and chug it. My shirt is drenched and clings to my body in a way I don't like. Luckily, this arena has showers just off our room, and I brought a change of clothes. I hop into a quick shower and get cleaned up. The water feels fantastic as it washes the sweat and adrenaline away. I return to the room and see Grayson sitting on a couch with Jack, Johnny, and Jose bottles. Also sitting with him are a bunch of girls in barely there clothing who are giggling like crazy as they hold red solo cups and make clumsy attempts at the sign Grayson is trying to teach them.

Maddie stands in the corner, her clipboard clenched tightly in her hand as she watches Grayson flirt with the girls. "Hey, Mads." I walk up to her and grab another glass of water. She jumps and pulls her eyes away from the couch.

"Oh. Hey, Jensen. Here is your phone. I grabbed it from the locker on my way back." I take it from her and thank her. I nod toward the couch. "What's with Barbie, Bimbie, and company?"

Maddie rolls her eyes so hard I fear she will hurt herself. "They were waiting outside the entry with the alcohol. I would have security remove them, but Grayson said they could come in." One of the girls, I'm not sure which, lets out a loud peal of annoying laughter. Maddie wrinkles her nose. "I'm going to head back to check on things on the stage side. Delilah is there waiting on Gio. Let me know when I can take the trash out." She stalks out of the room, closing the door with more force than usual. Grayson looks up at the vibrations, and I shake my head.

Grabbing my phone, I flip to Lily's messages. She loved the picture of the sound check, but I haven't heard anything else from her, so I shoot off a quick text.

Hey angel baby, we just got off stage! How was your day?

I set my phone aside, grab a plate, and load it with the sandwiches and chips. I love sandwiches. They are honestly my favorite food. You can make a sandwich out of just about any-thing. When I was little, much to my dad's dismay, I would but-ter bread and put spaghetti in it. The thought has me unlocking my phone again and texting Dad. He writes back immediately; he was probably waiting by the phone to hear how my night went. We chat for about forty-five minutes, and Lily did not text back.

I hear the crowd roar from here, so I head back toward the stage. Gio is doing an encore, pulling Delilah back on stage with him. I stand in the shadows and watch them shining under the stage lights, both in their element. The song ends, and Delilah takes a short bow before being hauled into Gio's arms and kissed soundly. The noise that follows has me covering my ears. That will be on VidReel before I get back to the bus.

Delilah grins as she and Gio head back to our rec room; her shriek tells me she made it. The three girls from the room rush past me. Two are holding their shirts to their front. My eyebrows hit my hairline, and I hustle back to the room to see Delilah giving Grayson the chewing out of his life. I didn't know she knew so many signs, but the way Maddie is still interpreting tells me Delilah is so mad she's getting a lot of it wrong. Something Delilah signs must be funny because Grayson starts to laugh and then has to desperately try to protect his head from the pillow Delilah is now brandishing.

"Delilah! You got the sign wrong! Delilah!" Maddie tries grap-pling with Delilah to get the pillow away from her. Her words must register because Delilah suddenly lets go of the pillow, sending Maddie flying backward to land in Grayson's lap. Shoving her glasses back onto her face correctly, she scrambles to get up.

"What?" Delilah looks at Maddie like she's never seen her before.

"You signed it wrong." Maddie is calmer now that Delilah isn't beating Grayson with a pillow. She adjusts her glasses again before tucking her hair behind her ear.

"Well, what did I sign then?" Delilah crosses her arms in irritation.

"Oh. Um. You signed don't be a donkey, stop dancing girls, while I am pretty sure you meant don't be dumb, stop chasing girls, which is very similar. That's why Grayson laughed. Even though he is a bit of an ass." Maddie mutters the last bit. I only hear it because I'm standing behind her and bust out laughing.

"Oh. Well. Okay then, but still." She points a finger at Grayson. "I don't want to see any more dumb bimbos in my rec room."

At that moment, Mia walks in, already showered and changed. Her long black hair hangs wet down her back. She's got a note card in her hands. "Hey, did y'all see anyone near the lockers?"

I glance at the others but shake my head. "I didn't stop by the lockers. Maddie grabbed my phone for me."

We all look at Maddie. "There were many people back there when I grabbed Jensen's phone, but I didn't see anyone looking out of place. What happened?"

Mia waves the note card in the air. "Someone left a note in my locker. It isn't signed, and it's a bit weird."

I take the note and open it.

"You were beautiful on stage but would look better in my bed. Soon, my love."

"Wow. Well. That's... yeah, that's fuckin creepy." I hand the note back. "You should tell someone about that."

"Oh, it's probably just a stagehand. I'm not going to worry about it too much. Are we ready to get out of here?"

Grayson grabs two bottles, holding them up triumphantly before heading toward the bus. Delilah and Gio head back to his bus, and we head back to ours. In only a matter of minutes, we are on the road to our next stop.

Chapter Thirty

Lily

Wild Child Reckless has been opening for Gio Santorro for two months, playing several shows a week. This week, they're in Hartford, Connecticut, about two hours from where I'm staying. I didn't tell Jensen I'd come because I wasn't sure with midterms, but I finished early, and Marco offered to drive me. I texted Delilah to help me surprise Jensen, and she's leaving tickets and backstage passes at will call. The energy is palpable, and the crowd is mostly screaming girls. Marco helps me avoid getting jostled in the packed venue.

As the lights dim and the first chord hits, I feel the shift. This isn't the same band that played at Havenbrook Square—this is bigger, sharper, and more polished. Wild Child Reckless was always good, but now they're great. The lights go up, and I spot Jensen. My breath catches—he's changed. He looks leaner, harder, with his hair flopping over his forehead. He's more confident, maybe cocky, working the stage with Delilah. Judging by the crowd's reaction, I can't tell if his transformation is good or bad.

"Isn't that your brother?" Marco leans in.

"Stepbrother. Yeah, Jensen." I watch as they transition into the next song. Jensen tosses a guitar pick into the crowd, pulls out another, and doesn't miss a beat.

"He's good," Marco says.

I nod, speechless. After almost an hour, the band finishes and heads off stage. I motion for Marco to stay and enjoy the encore as I head backstage. Security stops me, but I flash my pass and get through.

I am wandering around looking for Jensen when I run into Delilah.

"Lillian! There you are! I was about to look for you. I'd stick around, but I have to play the encore with Gio. Jensen's inside; he's been talking about his Christmas trip nonstop," she says with a grin before heading off.

I approach the door she pointed to and hear laughter inside. I hesitate, then walk in—and immediately want to walk out. Grayson's on a couch with two drunk girls, and Jensen—my Jensen—is sitting with a brunette on his lap, whispering to her as he grips her hip.

I must make a noise because Jensen's eyes snap to mine, widening as he pushes the girl off.

"Angel baby!" he calls, reaching for me, but I back out, shutting the door. Tears well in my eyes as I fumble for my phone to text Marco.

"Lily!" Jensen shouts behind me. I swipe at my tears and turn to face him.

"What, Jensen?" I snap, trying to hide how much I'm hurting.

"Angel baby, nothing happened! I didn't even invite them; Grayson did."

"You didn't invite them, but you sure looked cozy with her on your lap," I say, cutting him off. "Is this why you've been distant? Is this what happens after every show?" Images of him partying with girls flood my mind, and it's worse knowing that's what he's been doing while I've been sitting at home, studying and waiting for a text. Rage bubbles inside me.

I knock his hand away when he reaches for me just as Marco arrives.

"What's going on here? I got your text," Marco says, his gaze hardening when he sees I've been crying. "Who is this, and why are you making Lily cry?"

"It's a misunderstanding. Who are you, and how'd you get back here?" Jensen asks, bristling.

"I'm Marco. Lily texted me and said she was ready to leave. She came with me." His tone is casual, but it's like waving a red flag at a bull.

"You came together?" Jensen looks at me, begging me to deny it, but I can't. We did.

"Yes. Marco wanted to see the show, and I wanted to see you. My car's still in Texas. Marco drove me here in exchange for a ticket."

Jensen clenches his jaw. "Marco, huh? I've heard of you."

Marco checks his phone, looking bored. "That's nice. I haven't heard of you."

I gasp and scuttle backward as Jensen throws a punch. Marco doesn't hit back; he just puts Jensen in a hold he struggles to break. Marco releases him and shoves him away. "Don't be silly. You're going to hurt yourself. Besides, it's not good for Lily to be around this. Get yourself under control."

Marco straightens his shirt, fixing his hair as he chides Jensen.

"Jensen!" Several workers help Jensen up, and I rush to his side.

"What is *he* doing here?" I recoil at his harsh tone—he's never spoken to me like this before.

"*He* drove me here to see *you*. I wanted it to be a surprise." I can't hide the hurt in my voice. If Jensen notices, he doesn't show it, still glaring at Marco.

"You're blowing this out of proportion. Marco's been nothing but respectful."

"I'm sure he has." The sarcasm drips from Jensen's words.

"Why are you being like this? I don't understand! You don't have the right to be upset. I come all the way to see you, and I walk in to find a half-dressed... floozy on your lap, but you're upset with *me*?"

"I told you, nothing happened—"

"And I told you Marco has been nothing but respectful!" I interrupt. Jensen scoffs, and I throw my hands up in frustration. "Is this how it's going to be? You ignore me for groupies, and I can't even have one friend where I know no one else? Am I just supposed to sit at home and wait for you to have time for me?"

"Angel baby—" His tone, once comforting, now makes me want to scream—so I do. Technicians swarm us, trying to defuse the situation.

"No." I point a shaking finger at him. "No, you don't get to throw a fit and act like I'm the unreasonable one. I've spent two months waiting—for a text, a picture, anything. You're living your dream, and I'm drowning in silence. You were light and color, and you brought me back to life." I wipe away tears. "I just didn't realize you chasing your dream would mean the end of mine."

Marco walks up behind me and puts a hand on my shoulder. I glance at him, and he nods toward the exit. I nod back.

"Lily." I stop and close my eyes at the pain in his voice.

"I can't do this, Jensen. I thought I was stronger, but I'm not. I can't sit on the sidelines waiting for any scrap of attention and affection you can show me. It isn't fair to you or me. You deserve to ride this dream as far as it will take you, and I deserve someone who is there for me." I start toward the exit.

"Lily, I love you."

I stumble to a stop. Jensen has never said those words in all our years together. They were implied every day but never declared. I turn to see him standing there, and I see a glimpse of the boy who stole my heart in the man he's starting to become. Marco grabs my hand as I turn to walk back, but I shake my head.

Jensen folds me close to his body, and I can't deny that it feels like home even now. We stand there for a minute which lasts hours.

I sniffle and wipe the tears away again before patting his chest. "It's not enough, Jensen, and we were foolish to think it would be. This is your dream." I gesture to the stadium around us. "I can't compete with this. I never could. No matter how much I love you." I whisper the last words for his ears only, and he inhales sharply, pulling me tighter to his body.

I step away, walking backward. I mouth "I love you" one last time before I turn and let Marco lead me out of the exit. The roar of the crowd is drowned out by the shattering of my heart.

Two months later, Christmas is here, and I'm standing at the base of our tree waiting. I don't know why I'm here except for some misguided hope that he would show up. I know from Michael that he is touring the West Coast, but there was hope the band would return for the holiday.

He didn't show.

Chapter Thirty-One

Jensen- One Year Later

Touring as the headliner is entirely different from touring as an opening act. It's addicting. It's everything I ever wanted. Wild Child Reckless is bigger than ever, and aside from my grandparents' pesky lawyer, life is perfect. So why am I pacing beneath this magnolia tree, my breath steaming in the winter air?

I lean back against the trunk and kick back, staring out across the field. Memories play in my head like a movie scene. Sighing, I push off and head back to my truck.

She didn't show.

Chapter Thirty-Two

Lily- One Year Later

Sighing, I walk up to the magnolia tree, standing bare in the winter sun. Winter in Texas is far different than in Boston, so I am glad. Thinking back to my first real winter, I am still unsure how I survived. Hot chocolate helped, of course, but the amount of ice and snow was and still is mind-boggling. My text tone beeps, and I stare down at my phone to see a message from my father.

You will marry him, Lillian. Don't try me, girl. You know what will happen if you do.

The phone goes back into my pocket, and I lean against the trunk of the tree, uncaring about the snags in my latest designer jacket. I never thought about what my life would be like after school. I guess part of me was still naive to the lengths my father would go to gain power. Now it has been decided that Marco and I will be married. I thought it was a joke at first. Marco was a constant over the last four years in Boston. I count him as a good friend. Which is why I thought it was a joke when he warned me about what his father and mine had come up with.

Joke's on me.

I hear a door closing, and I turn to see Marco making his way to me. While I knew the chances of it being Jensen were slim to none, part of me was still hopeful that he would save me again.

"Lily?" Marco has reached me, and I turn to look at him as he stands there. "Are you ready to go now? We promised your mother that we wouldn't be gone long. They were waiting for us to start dinner." I nod quietly and let him take my hand to lead me back to our rental car.

Maybe being married to Marco won't be that bad. After that disastrous concert in Hartford, I spilled everything to him on the drive back to my apartment in Boston. He listened the whole way. He told me Jensen was a fool and that I deserved better. Then, he proceeded to pick up all my favorite comfort foods.

"Lily?"

I shake my head, pulling myself out of my thoughts. "I'm sorry, Marco. Yes. Let's go." I smile at him, and he smiles back but is clearly worried.

"Lily, are you sure? Why are we here?"

My smile is sad when I reach the waiting car as he opens the door for me. "It doesn't matter. He didn't show."

Chapter Thirty-Three

Jensen- One Year Later

I take a swig from the bottle, feeling the familiar burn settle in my stomach. These days, drinking is the only thing that makes me feel anything. Delilah's tried to talk to me, worried, but I keep brushing her off. She's so wrapped up in Alexander that I don't worry about her disapproval anymore. Wedding preparations have a way of distracting even the most vigilant brides.

I glance at my phone, reading the headline again: *Southern Charm Meets Corporate Clout: Governor's Daughter Lassoed by Business Tycoon's Heir!* The article gushes about the upcoming Christmas wedding in New York, with details about bridal parties and famous guests. Below it is a black-and-white photo of Lily standing next to Marco. A growl builds in my chest. Marco. I should've kicked his ass when I had the chance. I zero in on Lily's smile—it's her fake one, the polite mask she wears when hiding her true feelings.

I take another swig and hurl the bottle at the wall. I have to get out of here. Grabbing my keys, I head to the garage, pressing the fob to locate my car—a 1969 Chevrolet Camaro SS. When we got our first big check from touring, I bought it and had it tricked out. My dream car; the one dream I could make real. I find it and slide into the driver's seat. I need to get out. The memories are too much and the booze isn't numbing them like usual.

The muscle car roars to life, and I peel out of the parking spot. I don't know where I'm going, but it doesn't matter. I take the first right, aiming for the interstate. A few blocks later, red and blue lights flash behind me.

"Fuck." I slam my hand against the wheel and pull over. This isn't good—Delilah might actually kill me. I reach for my phone to call Maddie. If anyone can keep this quiet, it's her.

The clang of the cell doors a while later makes me curse under my breath. The officer booked me for DUI, then had the nerve to ask for an autograph. Sure, he's a fan, but I'm still sitting in this damn cell.

"Well, if I knew this was all it took to find you, I'd have done it sooner. You're a hard man to track down, Mr. Parker." The voice belongs to a tall, lean man in an expensive custom suit. "I am Jude Snyder, esquire."

"Well, Mr. Snyder—no offense, but who the fuck are you?" My hands are already shaking. I would kill for a drink right now. Lily's engaged, I'm in a jail cell, and I have no idea how to keep this from blowing up in the tabloids.

"I've been trying to reach you for a while." He hands me a business card. I glance at it.

"Let me guess—trying to contact me about my car's extended warranty?"

He chuckles. "Not quite. I'm here on behalf of your mother." My head snaps up, and I glare at him so hard he takes a step back.

"I want nothing to do with my grandparents. Nothing." I tear the card in half and drop it.

He sighs. "I'm not here for them. In fact, they'd probably prefer I wasn't here at all. I'm here on behalf of your late mother. She hired me to manage her estate until you came of age. You've refused every meeting and rejected all the mail I've sent. This is not my usual method, but given your... avoidance, I didn't have much choice."

He pulls some folded documents from his coat pocket and passes them through the cell bars. "Your mother set up a trust for you in the event of her death, structured in such a way—thanks largely to me—that your grandparents haven't been able to uncover the full extent of it."

I unfold the documents and start reading. When I reach the financial section, I whistle.

"Ah, yes. The trust also includes controlling ownership of your grandparents' company, which is probably why they've been eager to determine what would happen to your mother's shares."

"Wait, what?" I can hardly believe it. Not only do I have more money than I'll ever need, but I also own my grandparents' company? It seems too good to be true, but it is in black and white.

"Yes, it's hard to believe, but it's true. Let's get you out of here, sobered up, and start the paperwork." I watch as he walks away, shaking my head as I scan the documents again. What else is today going to throw at me? Fifteen minutes later, I'm back on the sidewalk with all charges dropped. I glance around at the bustling crowd but don't see any paparazzi or even a phone aimed at me.

"If you're looking for paparazzi, you won't find any. This won't make tomorrow's crime report." Jude stands next to me, adjusting his cuff. I can't help but stare.

"How'd you manage that?" He smiles and shrugs, and I laugh. "Okay, keep your secrets. Now, about the paperwork?"

"Yes, let's head to the hotel. Hopefully, maid service has cleaned your room." A black sedan pulls up, and Jude gestures for me to enter. "Antoine, the hotel, please. Thank you."

An hour later, everything is signed, notarized, and on its way to be filed. "Now, regarding your shares, you might want to appoint a board of directors. A conservatory or management company could handle daily affairs if that doesn't appeal to you. Of course, you could always sell your shares—your grandparents have tried for years to get them, so I'm sure they'd be eager to buy."

"I can't begin to describe how little interest I have in running a company." Jude chuckles, and I take another sip of my white mocha. "However, I am unsure if I want to sell them yet. Do I need to make that decision today?"

Jude flips through the paperwork but shakes his head. "No, you don't have to make a decision today. Once it gets out that we've filed the paperwork, people will come out of the woodwork trying to bend your ear for investment opportunities. I am certain that the minute your grandparents find out, you will receive a buyout offer. Once that happens, you must decide, but until then, we can coast."

"I don't plan on investing in anything anytime soon. However, if I do, would you be available for consultation?" Touring with the band, I was not hurting for money before today's revelation; however, now that I have money on an epic scale, it is more than a little intimidating.

"Of course. I am happy to stay on as a consultant for as long as you require. My fees can continue to be paid out of the estate. This can be adjusted at any time. If you need nothing else from me, I think I will head back to Savannah. I have been away for far too long." Jude stands, but I stop him with a hand on his arm.

"Actually, there is one more thing. Are you able to hire someone to look into someone for me?" I can feel an idea forming.

"You mean like a private investigator? Yes, I know several good ones that should be available. Who do you want looked into?" Jude opens his notebook, pulling a pen from his jacket pocket.

"Marco. Marco Russo." I will only convince Lily to leave this jerk if I can prove he isn't who she thinks he is. This means I need everything I can get on him. "While you do that. I am going to New York."

"New York? What are you going to do in New York?" Jude looks at me like I've grown two heads.

"I'm gonna win back my girl."

Chapter Thirty-Four

Lily

The camera flash is bright as the photographer takes another photograph, fluttering around us like a cracked-out hummingbird with high beams. I hurry and shove a massive bite of cake in my mouth while her back is turned. Marco chuckles, turning to speak into my ear. "Hungry?"

I hurry up and swallow so I can reply. "Starving. We have been sitting here with all these cakes being photographed for *hours*. If I am going to be forced to go through with this wedding, no offense, then I am damn well going to eat some cake! You better prepare yourself. You may end up with a fat bride after all of this!"

"Do you realize it's been forty-five minutes, tops?" I glare at him, and he smiles back.

"That's not the point. Who goes to a cake tasting to be photographed? I want to eat cake at a cake tasting!" I know I am being whiney, and I can't help. Blame it on low blood sugar.

"Okay, okay. Let's eat some cake, shall we?" He forks up a bite of the double chocolate caramel fudge cake I was eyeing and holds it to my mouth. I take the offered bite, only to be blinded again by the photographer.

"Oh, that is just the sweetest! Can you do it again?" She flutters around us as Marco dutifully feeds me bites of all the different cakes, humor lighting his light brown eyes. I smile back and take each bite. To anyone on the outside looking in, we are the picture of a couple in love. If anyone were even to suspect the truth…things would not end well for anyone involved. Marco wipes a crumb from my bottom lip. I follow his thumb with my tongue. Heat flares in his eyes, and I quickly pull back.

"Are we done here?" I turn to look at the photographer before pushing back from the table and standing. She stammers something affirmative, and I head to let the baker know which cake I picked. Marco walks up behind me, wrapping an arm around my shoulders. I lean against him, and he kisses my temple warmly.

"I'm sorry. I didn't mean to upset you."

I sigh as he takes my hand, and we head out of the pâtisserie. "I know. It wasn't that. It's just that I don't want you to get the wrong idea." I still feel horrible. Marco is, despite his familial connections, a wonderful person. I am lucky to have spent the last four years with him as a friend. If given the chance, he would welcome a change in our relationship. An opportunity to leave the friend zone, if you will. However, he knows that only one man will ever hold the keys to my heart. Unfortunately for me, that man has spent the last four years whoring himself across the country and then getting engaged to his best friend.

"Trust me, котик. I am under no illusion about where I stand in your heart's affection. No, no, no." He stops me with a finger against my lips. "I do not tell you this to make you feel guilty. I am simply stating a fact." He tucks me next to his body as we head to the parking garage. "Where to next?"

I check the agenda we received from the wedding planner. "Well, we have a tasting with the catering company in an hour and then a venue tour. Tomorrow is dress shopping—complete with a photographer—so that should be a blast." We reach the town car, and Marco opens my door for me.

"Well, if we have an hour, why don't we do something fun? What do you think—shoes, books, or coffee?" I settle into the plush leather seat, bouncing with excitement.

"Why don't we have coffee and books? There are several new releases that I want to grab. If we go to Barnes and Noble on East 17th, we can grab coffee and books and still be close to the caterer's and the Manhattan penthouse for the first venue appointment." I buckle my seatbelt as Marco slides behind the wheel.

"Whatever my котик wants, she gets." His hand is warm as he holds mine, kissing my knuckles before starting the car and pulling into traffic. The radio is comfortable, and we sit in companionable silence as we go through the start-and-stop traffic only New York offers.

When we finally reach Barnes and Noble, I immediately go to the coffee kiosk and order my venti White Chocolate Frappuccino with extra whip and two additional shots. Caffeinated and ready, I grab a basket and head straight to the romance section. Mia Fury has a new shifter series that I want to add to my collection. Morgan Elliott has a new installment in her Mafia series: *Lethal Submission*. I walk around sipping my coffee happily until Marco taps my shoulder.

"котик, we have to go, or we are going to be late. Did you find everything you needed?" He takes the basket from me, grunting slightly at the heft.

"Needed? I needed them all. I can always find something I need at Barnes and Noble! I saw something for you too." I pull out a book with a gorgeous purple-and-pink cover. "It's called *Finding Poetry, Finding Me*. It's by a new indie poet named Rebecca Bruckenstein. I flipped through them, and they are pretty good. I thought you might enjoy the poems. We're almost through the last book we bought."

Marco takes the book from me and reads the back before rewarding me with his megawatt smile. "Thank you, котик. You always amaze me with your sweetness. We have to hurry, though; let's go." We check out and return to the car just before my phone rings.

"Father." I roll my eyes before answering the call with forced cheerfulness. "Hello, Father. We are on our way to the caterer's. What can I do for you?"

"Lillian. Hello. You were supposed to message the wedding planner your cake choice after the tasting. You did pick a cake, correct?" I sigh.

"Yes, Father. We picked the double chocolate caramel cake for the groom's cake and the Chantilly cream cake for the bridal cake. They will coordinate with the florist to get me a selection of live flowers for decoration. I didn't message the wedding planner because she was at the tasting with us." I can't keep the irritation out of my voice. It is bad enough I am being forced to go through with this wedding sham, but the micromanaging is getting too much. Marco deftly removes my phone from my hand.

"Forgive me, Mr. DuPont, but we are at the caterer's, and I can see the planner waiting for us. We will make sure she has the cake selections notated. Yes, yes. Of course. Father said he would be back in the country later this week. Naturally. До встречи." Marco hangs up the call and rolls his eyes. "Your father could make a priest swear." I giggle and take my phone back, sliding it into my purse.

I'm still giggling when Marco approaches my door, helping me exit the car. "I feel so much better. Thank you. You have taken a frustrating day and turned it completely around." I loop an arm around his waist and hug him tightly, something he gladly returns. "Now, let's go see about this food."

Chapter Thirty-Five

Jensen

According to Google, Kleinfeld Bridal in Chelsea is a world-renowned 35,000-square-foot luxury bridal salon, famous for its appearance on *Say Yes to the Dress.* I managed to bribe my way inside. I arrived in New York last night and rented a room at the Hyatt House New York Chelsea, just half a mile from the shop. My only plan was to get into Lily's dress appointment. This might be my last chance to speak to her alone.

"Good afternoon, Ms. DuPont. I'm Charlotte, your consultant today. Per your father's instructions, we've selected a few gowns: the Pnina Tornai Couture Ball Gown, the Allure Bridals A-Line, and the Verdin Bridal Floral Ball Gown. Let me know if you need assistance." Charlotte, the consultant I bribed earlier, doesn't follow Lily into the changing room. I hide behind the curtain, holding my breath.

Lily enters, drops her purse, and closes her eyes like she's praying for patience. She begins unbuttoning her blouse. The more skin she reveals, the less comfortable my jeans feel. I tap her shoulder—probably not the smartest move. Lily screams, clutching her blouse and backing away.

"котик? Are you okay?" Her panic subsides when she recognizes me. I gesture for her to stay quiet. Her eyes narrow, but she's distracted by the turning doorknob.

"I'm fine! Sorry, this dress is stunning. I'll be out in a moment, darling!" Her glare tells me I'm in trouble.

"Angel baby," I say, watching her. She's grown into such a woman. Her waist-length blonde curls now have lighter streaks, giving her an ethereal glow. Her style is still wealthy but more personal now, unlike back in Texas. I'm so distracted that I don't see her swing. She clocks me upside the head.

"Jesus, Lily! What the hell?"

"That's for scaring me! What are you doing here? And how did you even get in?" She looks around the room like someone else might be hiding.

"Who are you looking for?" I glance around with her.

"Anyone else hiding!" She throws up her hands in frustration, and I chuckle.

"There's no one else. Honestly, the fact that I have to hide just to talk to you is a bit disconcerting." I move her purse and sit in the chair as she glares. I just grin—this is more fun than I expected.

"Jensen, you need to leave. I have to try on these dresses for the photographer. They'll wonder where I am."

I stand and pick up a dress, handing it to her. "Don't let me stop you. A bit... poofy for my taste, but if you like it, Angel baby." I sit again, crossing my legs.

"Jensen! I can't try on wedding dresses with you sitting there watching!" She looks scandalized, which makes me grin more.

"Why not? It's nothing I haven't seen before. Though, I always thought the first time I saw you in a wedding dress would be walking down the aisle to me. But hey, I'll take a sneak preview. Because if you think you're marrying anyone else, you're mistaken."

Lily growls in frustration, and I settle in.

She stomps her foot, frustrated, then sheds her blouse. A pale pink corset hugs her skin. The skirt follows, and adult Lily has traded her teenage boy shorts for a thong. She grabs the dress off the hanger, struggling to get it over her head. I stand to help, and she bats my hands away after we manage it. I laugh as she finally gets a good look at herself. "You look like a cupcake on steroids."

Lily turns to the mirror, holding back laughter. "More like a snow beast. I'd better let them get their pictures." She steps out, and the chorus of 'oohs and aahs' from the viewing area has me shaking my head. The photographer's directions are ridiculous, but Lily doesn't complain.

Fifteen minutes later, she returns, steps out of the gown, and grabs another. "What was all that?" I hang the dress as she picks a new one.

"Father hired a photographer to document all the wedding events: cake tasting, catering, dress shopping, everything. It's frustrating, but what can I do?"

I stare at her. "You say no. It's a full sentence. You're not unfamiliar with it—you say it to me all the time."

She rolls her eyes, slipping into a sleeker dress, which is a vast improvement. She twirls in the mirror, catching my eye. "I don't always tell you no, Jensen. Why are you here anyway? Shouldn't you be off whoring—sorry, touring?"

I don't miss the resentment in her voice. I shrug. "I haven't been a saint, but can you tell me you haven't had your share of fun in the last four years?"

Lily stops spinning, staring at the floor, a blush creeping over her cheeks.

"Angel baby." I approach her, turning her to face me. "Do you mean to tell me you—" She throws my hands off and steps back.

"It's not a big deal, okay?" She turns her back, defensive.

"You're getting married. I just assumed—"

"Yeah, and we all know what assuming does, don't we?" Lily's blush deepens as she hugs herself.

"Right, I just—"

She shoots me a glare. "Yes, Jensen, I know. Some of us see intimacy as more than sharing our bodies. We share our whole selves." She turns to leave. "When I get back, I want you gone."

The door slams, and I grimace. This isn't going how I pictured it. My phone beeps with an email. The investigator Jude hired has sent the report on Marco. I need to look at it as soon as possible. I grab a receipt from my pocket and scribble a note to Lily asking her to meet me at my hotel room later this evening. I also add my new cell phone number before slipping out the back. I should have plenty of time to review the report before Lily arrives.

Three hours later, a knock on my door pulls me from my whiskey. I set the tumbler down and open the door to find Lily shifting nervously and gripping her purse as if someone might steal it.

"Lily. Angel baby. I didn't know if you'd come. Please, come in." I step back, holding the door open as she walks into the sitting area. "Can I get you something to drink? Wine? Water? Whiskey?" I raise my glass before downing the rest in one gulp.

"I'll take a Pellegrino, thanks." I check the minibar, pull out a bottle, and hand it to her as she sits on the sofa.

"Lily, I've been thinking about what you said earlier." I pour another drink and sit in the recliner, watching her closely. "You said you couldn't say no to your father about this marriage. Some might assume you love your fiancé, but the fact that you haven't been with anyone since we split makes me think you don't love Marco as much as you've led everyone to believe."

I grab the papers I printed from the business center and slap them onto the coffee table between us. "The report from my private investigator confirms my hunch."

Lily stares down at the papers on the table before reaching down and spreading them out, glancing at each page before stacking them back up. "Your investigator is quite excellent and worth whatever you are paying him. However, he missed one vital piece of information."

Lily's cool tone only enrages me more. "What exactly is that?"

Lily takes a sip of her water before looking right at me and replying, "I still said yes."

Chapter Thirty-Six

Lily

I see Jensen's jaw clench from the sofa, and I shake my head. He may look grown up, but he's still the same hot-headed boy from Havenbrook.

"You don't love him," Jensen grits out, and I can only nod.

"I don't love him, but he's a good man."

Jensen scoffs. "The report says otherwise. His father owns both legal and illegal businesses. He's been indicted—though never convicted—for gun running across the border, among other things. Marco is set to inherit and has been preparing for five years. I haven't even touched on your father's involvement."

Hearing my father is tied to Vincent Russo's shady dealings doesn't surprise me. Marco told me early on that his father's business wasn't exactly clean. Marco wants to shift it toward legal ventures when he takes over.

"I'm sure your report is thorough. But Marco has never hidden who he is or what his family does from me. He's always been honest, and more than that, he's always been there for me. He's as trapped in this marriage as I am. The only difference is, he wishes it could be more."

"So what you're saying is you don't love him."

"You're like a dog with a bone, you know that, right? Must you hear me say it? No. No, I don't love Marco. There. Are you happy now?" I throw my hands up in frustration. The next thing I know, Jensen leans over me and presses me back onto the couch.

"You don't love him, but you do love me." His tone is smug, and I have to roll my eyes.

"Jensen, I don't even know you anymore. I loved the boy you were once, but you are not that boy anymore. Frankly, what I know about the man you have become makes me think you should be showering with bleach because there are some things that soap won't wash off, and you don't seem to have been very careful."

Jensen laughs a big, booming laugh, and I can't help but smile in return. "I can assure you, angel baby, I have nothing that won't be washed off with soap. Your concern, though, that's very touching." Jensen sits beside me on the couch, pressing his body against mine. "Now that I know you do not love Marco, I no longer feel guilty about breaking up your wedding and keeping you for myself."

"Jensen, you cannot do that." I gasp in fear, knowing that if my father even got a hint of a plan like this, he would rain hell down on Mike and Mom. "I know you are used to getting your way, but this affects more than just you and me. Please. You can't do this. I have to marry Marco."

"Because if you don't, then your father threatened to use his power to mess with Dad, your mom, and our families. Yes, I know that too. My guy was very, very thorough. Also, it turns out your father doesn't treat his employees very well and more than a few are willing to testify." I sit there and stare at him, not fully comprehending what he is saying to me.

Jensen picks up his tumbler and takes another sip, watching me as I work through everything he has said to me. I could be free, free to live a life of my choosing. But one thing still bothers me.

"Why did you do all of this, and how did you afford it?"

Jensen grimaces. "Well, that's a two-part story. First, I started this because I didn't think I could convince you to leave Marco any other way. I wanted to prove he wasn't worthy of you. It was purely selfish—I admit that. As for your second question, I can afford all this because my narcissistic mother left me a ton of money and majority ownership in my grandparents' company. She hired a lawyer to manage it until I came of age. I spent the last four years avoiding him because I thought he worked for my grandparents."

I gape at him, shocked. He shrugs and takes another swig of whiskey. "My mother loved to play mind games. She would convince you that you were wrong and that she had never said something when you knew she had. She would twist and play the victim until you were convinced that you were going crazy. I'm not sure why she married my dad; I think as a big fuck you to her parents. She had a string of lovers my entire life and worked more than she was at home. Frankly, the fact that she left a trust for me was shocking. I always felt she didn't care about me; I didn't fit into the perfect little world she was trying to create."

Jensen gets up and strolls to the window to look over the New York City skyline, sipping his drink. "The day she died, she was out with her current boyfriend. She was drinking, and it was raining. She lost control and flipped her car; she was DOA. We spent a year in California before moving back to Texas so that Dad could help Abuela. My grandparents tried everything to find me in the beginning—we moved a lot that first year—but after that, they seemed to give up."

"That's when you moved to Havenbrook, met Delilah, and started the group."

Jensen nods before leaning back against the windows and looking at me on the couch. "She was so full of life, even at thirteen. I had the biggest crush on her for about a minute. Then, one day, I saw this blonde angel over a bonfire, and it felt like I couldn't breathe without her. When I found out she was going to be my stepsister, I didn't care—I just knew she was mine. But I broke it. I was young, stupid, and only saw the hurt. I tried to move on, but we were meant to be—the timing was just wrong."

Jensen moves to sit in front of me on the coffee table, clasping both of my hands in his. "What if that was the problem? We were too young; I was too prideful. I almost called you last

Christmas to hear your voice. I missed you so much. If you had answered, would we have picked up where we left off? We loved each other once, Lily. Could we do it twice?"

I sigh, pulling my hands back into my lap. "Jensen, loving you was never the problem. Those years together were ninety-nine percent perfect. But the fact that we couldn't make it work is a sign. I don't know if I can get over the last few years. Whenever I saw you in the paper or on TV with a different woman, it crushed me. How am I supposed to forget that?"

"By choosing me. By picking the good over the goodbye. I can't change what has happened, but I can make sure that from this moment to the end of my life, you never doubt that you are the one I need to complete my life. Without you, I have nothing. I am nothing. Do you want me to quit the group? Done. Do you want me to devote my life to following you worldwide? Done. I will gladly do anything you ask of me—anything but leave you. I've done it once and refuse to do it again."

I reach out and cup his cheek. My poor, poor Jensen. "Oh, Jensen. I would never ask you to give up the group. You love music."

"Not more than I love you. Ask me, Lily. Demand it. Yell. Rage. Slap me." Jensen gets to his knees before me, and I sit back to keep some space between us. "Anything. I will do anything to prove that we are meant to be."

I take a deep breath before taking his hands in mine. "Well then, I think there is only one thing that you can do."

"Anything. I will do anything. Just name it."

"You have to call Marco to come over."

Chapter Thirty-Seven

Jensen

If you had told me this morning that I would be willing to invite the man who is currently engaged to my girl to my hotel room, I would have accused you of being on drugs. However, that is the exact situation that I currently find myself in. Marco shuffles through the papers again before sitting them down.

"Do you know what you have here? Do you have any idea what you have done?" He slams back the finger of whiskey in his glass, so I give him another refill.

"I did what I had to do to ensure Lily was mine. We all need to decide what we do with that after today. The only thing I will not compromise on is that Lily must be protected at all costs."

Marco scoffs. "Like I would do anything to hurt Lily. During the last four years, all I have done has been to protect her. I was here day in and day out while you were off being гуляка. Do not come here and accuse me of being anything but devoted."

I stride up to him, and he rises to meet me. We stand there glaring at each other until small hands push against my chest.

"Dammit, Jensen. Please stop it. This is not going to help anything. Stop it, you two! This is not why we are here." Lily is frantically pushing against both of us, so I step back.

"Lily is right. This isn't why we are here. Now, I had my lawyer put out some feelers. You were already on more than a few agencies' radars. He's contacted one agent—Isabel Quinn— and she's willing to sit down off the record." Jensen tosses a business card down onto the table.

"What do you expect me to do with this? Betray my father? My family? You might as well be signing my death warrant. I wouldn't make it a week. There is no mercy for Стукач in the family." Marco sits back down, resting his arms on his knees and staring at the card on the table with a mixture of resignation and hope.

"Maybe you don't have to. I can turn over the paperwork I have. I can do it anonymously. We ensure you are not implicated in any wrongdoing—you would be arrested, sure—but we guarantee there is no way any of it could blow back on you. The information in that report would take down not only Lily's father but your own, leaving you free to continue legitimizing your father's holdings."

"It could work, but my father is Хитрец. He has slipped out from the consequences before." I've read the report. I know exactly what he means. This time, he may have more against him than he bargained for. It won't take much for Lily's father to roll over like a basketball.

"I don't think we will have any trouble getting charges to stick this time. I'll get with Jude about sending the papers to Agent Quinn. In the meantime, things will have to go on as usual. This includes your engagement party tomorrow night."

"How in the world do you know about that, Jensen?!"

I shrug. "I told you. My guy is really good. If I couldn't arrange to meet you at the bridal shop, my next chance would be at the engagement party."

"Wait. You were at the dress shop?"

I smirk at Marco's offended tone. "I sure was." Lily slaps my chest, and I can't help but laugh, pulling her close and kissing the top of her head. Marco watches the interaction before pulling Lily back to his side.

"We must go. It will look better if we leave together. Let me give you my number in case you need anything between now and then." He rattles it off, and I program it into my phone, texting him with my name. They head toward the door, and as I watch them go, my resolve wavers for just a moment. Maybe she would be better off if I were to let her go. She looks good next to him, and he obviously adores her. As if sensing my hesitation, Lily looks over her shoulder and meets my eyes.

"I'll see you tomorrow, angel baby." I wink at her, and her eyes widen in shock.

"Wait. You're still coming to the party?"

"I wouldn't miss it for the world."

"Jensen. I don't think this is a good idea." Jude lets himself into my hotel room with his key.

"Do you always walk into a room in the middle of a conversation?" Jude passes me the suit bag and shrugs.

"Possibly. I don't believe it's my fault if the other person is not listening. I got your suit, thirty-six long, as requested. However, I refuse to have you seen in anything as tacky as Jos A. Banks. I went with a Brioni. Thankfully, this is black tie because your tie collection is ghastly. You should burn them all." I can't help but laugh.

"Jude, are you a snob?"

Adjusting his cuffs, he glares at me. "I call it having good taste, something your wardrobe currently lacks." I laugh as I take the suit into the bathroom to change. "I contacted Agent Quinn and forwarded everything our guy found. You would have thought it was Christmas. She is coordinating with the other agencies. They could raid as soon as tonight, but they can't tell us for sure. Plausible deniability and all of that." Jude is pouring himself a drink when I walk out of the bathroom.

"I honestly don't want to know. How I view it is ignorance is bliss; I want to remain blissfully ignorant. What do you think?" I slowly turn, and Jude steps forward to straighten my lapels.

"Better. Now just let me see to the rest of your wardrobe, and I will be happy."

I shake my head. "You know your happiness matters to me, Jude." Sarcasm drips from my tone, but Jude nods.

"As it should." I snatch his glass from him and drain its contents before heading to the door.

"It's show time."

I pull up to the venue and hand my keys to the valet. Camera flashes explode as I smile and wave before heading inside. I'm recognized immediately and spend an hour mingling with dignitaries and celebrities. I have yet to see Lily or Marco. Still, Vincent and her father, Donald, are holding court at the back of the ballroom, surrounded by provocatively dressed women. I roll my eyes.

By my third whiskey, the emcee announces the couple. Lily descends the stairs on Marco's arm, stunning in a shimmering dress that sparkles like diamonds. Her blonde hair is swept into a complicated updo. She scans the room and smiles when she spots me. As they reach the bottom, the crowd surges forward. I retreat to the bar to watch and wait.

It doesn't take long—just a few hours. Donald approaches Lily, says something, and grabs her arm when she responds. I'm striding to her before I realize I even have moved. "You will remove your hand from her this instant." I'm just drunk enough not to care who hears me but sober enough to know that if push comes to shove, I can hand this man his ass.

"Jensen, it's okay. He didn't even hurt me, see? Just a little red. It's fine." Lily is trying to get me to go back and sit down, but that isn't going to happen. Not unless she is coming with me.

"I don't know who you think you are, young man, but I will speak to my daughter how I see fit." Donald snaps at security, and all I can see is red. I haul back and throw the most brutal punch I have ever thrown. I can feel his nose breaking under my knuckles. He squeals like a pig before hitting the floor. Security grabs my arms, but there is a sudden flash of light and several loud bangs as the room fills with smoke. People are screaming and running for the exits.

"Police! Hands up!"

I feel someone grab me, and I come around swinging, only to find myself face down on the ground, handcuffed. "Jensen!" Lily's cry runs through me like a live wire. She's scared. I struggle to flip around and kick out at the people holding me down. My only thought is to get to Lily, so I don't see the knock to my head coming until it is too late.

I wake up in a holding tank with a handful of men—most from the party if their attire is any indication. My head is killing me. I sit up and feel the back of my head. There is a softball-size knot, but there is no bleeding. I look up when Marco sits down next to me on the bench.

"She's safe. They got her out and took her to a secure location. They arrested quite a few people." I groan as I rub the back of my head again.

"I need to make a call. Jude has to know what's happened."

Marco points to the hallway. "An officer comes by about every fifteen minutes to check on everyone. He would be your best bet to make your phone call. Do you know Jude's phone number? They confiscated all electronic devices at the venue."

"Fuck. No. I don't have it memorized. But I do have something better. She may kill me when it's over and done with though." I grimace at the thought of making this call now.

"Who are you calling?" I stand up to the bars to see if I can find that officer.

"I'm gonna call Delilah."

Chapter Thirty-Eight

Lily

Jensen just punched Father when the first flashbang from the police explodes near us. The light is blinding, and I can only smell smoke. Someone grabs me from behind and leads me out of the house. I scream for Jensen, but I'm shoved into a car before I can find him. It's the most terrifying fifteen minutes of my life.

I'm taken to a room with basic amenities and left alone. Time crawls by. I'm too exhausted to sleep, so I splash water on my face and try to fix my hair. My once-elaborate updo now hangs limp. I pull out the pins and attempt a messy bun to keep it out of my face.

After what feels like days but is probably only hours later, I'm led into a room filled with agents. A woman with bright green eyes and long black hair introduces herself as Agent Quinn. She tells me they've been investigating Father and Vincent for over a year, and the information Jensen's investigator found was the last piece they needed for a warrant. I was cleared early in their investigation, and they only held me while they tied up the loose ends. They claim it was for my safety. I call bullshit.

As we talk, agents come and go, carrying boxes and equipment. I suddenly recognize one agent. "You!" I point at him, and the room goes quiet. "You were in my poli-sci class! You borrowed a pen." The agent looks sheepish. Overwhelmed, I ask, "What happens now?"

Agent Quinn explains, "We'll analyze everything we confiscated to build our case. You may be called in during the investigation, but we'll see."

"Can I go? I need to find Jensen, a bath, and a cheeseburger, in that order," I say, exhausted.

Agent Quinn frowns and checks her clipboard. "I don't have Jensen Parker listed here. Roark! Where's Parker?"

Roark glances up from his computer. "Looks like he's being held with the rest at the Manhattan Correctional Center."

I groan. Great.

Thirty minutes later, I'm in the precinct lobby, arguing with a portly deputy. "You will release him now, or I'll speak to your supervisor," I demand, infusing my voice with every bit of DuPont arrogance.

"Look, lady, he's being held without bail. There's nothing you or anyone can do about it."

I'm seconds from losing my temper when I hear a familiar voice from across the lobby. "Where is he? You will release him right now or so help me God!" Delilah Callahan (now Stephenson) storms into the lobby, and everything stops. I step back as she stomps up to the window, slamming her hands on the counter with enough force to rattle the pen cup.

"You listen to me, Deputy Donut. If you don't get off your deep-fried ass and find my best friend, I will make sure you are banned from every Krispy Kreme in the tri-state area."

"Now you look here!" The cop stands up, offended.

"No. You look here. I was on my honeymoon when I got the call from your facility. Now, how about you roll over to your supervisor—Lord knows it will be faster than you walking—and get me someone who knows how to do more than piss me off!" Alexander groans.

An older gentleman walks up to the window. "What seems to be the problem here?"

"The problem here is that Deputy Donut refuses to give me information about my best friend!" The new man sighs and clicks on the computer before looking back up.

"As my officer told your friend earlier, Mr. Parker is being held without bail. That is all the information I can give you." When he gestures to me, I shrink back under Delilah's ire.

Delilah rushes forward to hug me. "Lily! I didn't see you there! OMG, are you okay? Jensen didn't have a chance to tell me what was happening before they rushed him off the phone. I got here as soon as I could!"

Not hugging Delilah back is not an option, so I allow myself to be squeezed.

"Delilah, honey. You may wanna let her go so she can breathe." Alexander chuckles as Delilah jumps back.

"I am so sorry. So, what's up with Deputy Dumbass? He wouldn't tell you the charges either?"

I shake my head. "No. I was about to try to find Jensen's lawyer's number, but I no longer have a phone—it was confiscated." Delilah whips out her cell.

"What's his name?"

"Jude Snyder. I've never met him, but Jensen mentioned him a lot."

Her fingers fly over the screen before she holds the phone up to her ear. "Hello? Jude Snyder? It's Delilah—yes, that Delilah. No, no. Yeah, she's right here." Delilah glances at me. "No clue who that is. Got it. See you soon." She hangs up and pockets her phone. "Well, he's definitely interesting. He says he'll be here soon. He was waiting on a call from Jensen. I bet Jensen only called me because he couldn't remember anyone else's number. Idiot." We sit under the glaring stare of the desk deputy, waiting.

Ten minutes later, an impeccably dressed man strolls to the front desk. "Hello. Your phone is about to ring. I suggest you answer it." The phone on the desk immediately starts ringing. Deputy Donut stares at the man, down at the phone, and back up. "Go on. It's the governor. You don't want to keep him waiting."

The second Deputy Donut answers the phone, all hell seems to break loose. Cops are running back and forth, and Deputy

Donut is typing as if his life depends on it. Completely calm, the man walks over to us. "You must be Lily. It's lovely to make your acquaintance finally. I've heard wonderful things. You, of course, are Delilah. Delighted."

"What is happening?" I look around him at the scrambling cops.

"I just called some friends: Agent Quinn, the governor of New York. Turns out they were trying to charge Jensen with assaulting a peace officer and obstruction of justice. Which is completely ludicrous. They should be bringing him out any minute." The sound of a buzzer has us all standing to see a disheveled Jensen walking out.

"Jensen!" I run into his open arms and immediately burst into tears. Despite Jude's assurances, part of me worried I would never see him again.

"I'm here. I'm here. It's okay. I am here." The warmth of his arms around me chases away the chill. I can't hear the words he is murmuring, but just hearing his voice soothes something inside me.

"Jensen!" Another body rams into us as Delilah rushes forward. Jensen laughs and pulls her in close with us. We stand there for several minutes, just holding on to one another until a throat clears behind us.

Delilah walks back over to Alexander, and he pulls her against his side. "I'm glad to see you're no worse for wear, brother."

"Sorry about interrupting your honeymoon. They confiscated my phone and I couldn't remember anyone else's number." Delilah smacks Alexander on the stomach.

"I told you so!" We all laugh as Jude walks up to us.

"May I suggest we take this party elsewhere? The gentleman behind the partition has been glaring at you." Delilah turns and looks back.

"Who? Deputy Donut?"

Jensen chokes out a startled laugh as we all move toward the exit.

"I am starving. Let's find something to eat." Delilah turns on her heel and sashays out the door. We stare after her for a moment before busting out laughing and following her.

Chapter Thirty-Nine

Jensen

J ude declined to join us at the diner, claiming he had too much to do, though we teased him for it. Delilah and Lily are huddled together, laughing over wedding photos while eating fries. Then Lily gets a text from Marco saying both fathers are in custody and the cases are solid.

"I'm free," she whispers, then bursts into tears. I hold her as she cries into my shirt. We invite Marco to join us, but he declines, wishing Lily well and asking to be informed about the wedding. She blushes as she shows me the message, and I kiss her head.

"Tell him he's always welcome." I want to hate the man, but he kept her safe when I couldn't, and I owe him more than I can repay.

"I don't know what to do now," Lily says, her voice small. "Everything I own has been taken. I have nothing."

"You have me," I tell her. "I know I haven't always shown it, but I'm here now. Anything you want, say the word. Paris? Tomorrow. A new wardrobe? Here's my card. I'll do anything to prove I love you."

Delilah chimes in, "You have us," making Lily smile. I wipe her tears. "Ready for some sleep?" Delilah yawns, and we all laugh. After paying the bill, we hail a taxi, hug, and promise to meet after we rest.

Back at the hotel, the sun is rising. We haven't spoken since the diner. I hand Lily a shirt and shorts, and she smiles before disappearing into the bathroom. I quickly message Jude about phones and other essentials. I knock when I notice how long Lily has been in the shower. "Lily? You okay?" No response. I open the door, steam pouring out of the room. "Lily?" I call again, but all I hear is a sob. "Oh, angel baby. No." I rush into the bathroom to find her sitting on the tile, arms wrapped around her knees, as the hot water beats down on her from above. I cut off the water and grab a towel, wrapping it around her, and lift her into my arms. Setting her on the counter, I grab another towel and work on her hair. "Angel baby, it will be okay. I promise. Please don't cry. You're breaking my heart."

Once she is dry enough, I slip my shirt over her head. She dutifully puts her arms through. When I pick her up again, she wraps her arms and legs around me, burying her face in the crook of my neck. I head over to the bed and set her on the side so I can pull back the covers. I settle her back against the pillows and cover her up. I push the hair back from her face, cupping her cheek. "I'm going to shower quickly. Are you okay until I get back?" I ask her. She nods, sniffling loudly. I caress her cheek one last time before hurrying to take the fastest shower of my life. When I return to the room, Lily lies in bed staring out over the New York City skyline.

I slide under the covers beside her, and she gives me a small smile. "How are you feeling?" I'm more than a little worried.

"Foolish. Silly. Relieved. Lost." She chuckles, and I give her a small smile. "I know I should feel bad, and I know I should be worried about Father, but for so long, he was the monster in my closet, and all I can feel is relief." She sighs before continuing. "I'm also scared. I don't know who I am or what my life will be without him telling me."

"That's the beauty of it. You get to decide. You don't have to know today. You don't even have to know tomorrow. Sometimes, the best part of the journey is just enjoying the adventure." I tuck a wayward curl behind her ear. "I just want you to know that I would consider myself the luckiest guy on the planet if you would allow me to accompany you wherever your adventure takes you."

"Jensen, you were always my adventure. I never knew life could be as wonderful as it was when I was with you. I've missed you so much."

I tug her closer to me, and she settles against my chest. "There will be plenty of time for adventuring tomorrow. Go to sleep." I run my fingers through her hair, and she sighs, leaning into my hand. It takes a few minutes, but she finally falls asleep.

When I wake up, sunlight floods the room, and I immediately need coffee. Lily sleeps soundly beside me, so I slip out of bed, quietly ordering room service through the app. Whoever thought of that was a genius. After tidying up a bit, there's a knock at the door, and I tip the employee before moving the cart into the living room. Lily is sitting up in bed.

"Good morning! How'd you sleep?" I ask.

She smiles sheepishly. "So well, I forgot where I was when I woke up."

I hand her a cup of coffee and sit beside her. "I ordered a few dishes—pick whatever you like. And then, if you're up for it, how about an adventure?"

"An adventure?" She wrinkles her nose.

"Yeah, an adventure." I grin. "Do you trust me?"

She looks at me in surprise. "Do I trust you?"

"Do you?"

She scoffs. "You know I do. Where are we going?"

I take her hand. "Home."

I rented a private jet to take us back to Texas. The flight lasted four hours, and Lily was restless during the drive from Houston. When we crossed the county line, she could barely sit still.

"Slip this on," I say, holding out a blindfold. "I don't want to ruin the surprise."

She raises an eyebrow but agrees. As we turn onto the freshly graveled driveway, I can't help but smile. When I first bought this property, renovations were slow, but with nearly unlimited funds, mountains can be moved.

We pull up to the Winchester house, and even I'm impressed by the transformation. The white exterior sparkles in the sun, accented by dark blue shutters. It's not finished yet, but it's a work in progress—like us.

"Jensen? Can I look now?" Lily asks, tilting her head as if she can sense where we are.

"Just a second." I help her out of the car, leading her down the path. "Okay, now."

I remove the blindfold, and she blinks at the bright sunlight. When her eyes adjust, she gasps. "Jensen? Why are we at the Winchester house?"

"I thought you'd want to see the progress on our house—make sure everything's how you envisioned it."

Her gaze sweeps across the grounds, taking in the construction. "Our house?" she whispers.

I pull her close as we walk inside. She gasps again, tears streaming down her face as we explore. She stops when we reach the kitchen, stripped down to the studs.

"I have a designer ready to help you pick cabinets and fixtures. There were too many options for me to guess what you'd want. Are you okay?"

She stares out the kitchen window, silent. I follow her gaze and realize she's looking at our tree, which is perfectly visible from this point in the house. I hadn't noticed that before.

"You did this for me?"

I pull her close to me, resting my head on her. "I bought this house after our first tour. I couldn't afford to renovate more than a few things a year. Then, when I met Jude, I expedited the process. There are still a lot of decisions to be made that didn't feel right for me to make without you."

Lily sniffles. "I can't believe you did this, Jensen!"

I chuckle. "There is one more surprise." I lead her up the stairs to the master bedroom. I told them to focus on this and the en suite first. The walls are pale cream, and the furniture is dark mahogany. "Anything you don't like here can be changed, but I wanted us to have a comfortable place to stay while we pick out the rest of the house's features. Also, this way, we can spend time together away from the parents."

Lily walks around the room, stopping to smell the random candle someone, probably the designer, left on the dresser. The longer the silence, the more nervous I feel.

"Do you like it?" I can't help the wariness in my voice. The answer to this innocent question means everything.

Chapter Forty

Lily

I stare around the room and smell the candle again—Whispers of Spring. How appropriate. I still don't know what to think about Jensen buying and renovating our dream home. I have loved this home for so long. It feels surreal that I am standing in the master bedroom right now. I am overwhelmed in the best possible way. I calmly set the candle on the dresser before walking into Jensen's arms.

"I love you," I whisper into his chest, but he still hears me and pulls me tight against him.

"I have always and will always love you, Lillian Grace DuPont."

I can't help but stretch up on my tippy toes and press my lips to his. Jensen pauses in shock for a moment before taking over the kiss. His tongue teases my lips, and I open them eagerly, our tongues dueling for dominance in our haste.

Growling, Jensen picks me up and puts me back against the wall. I wrap my legs around his waist, and I can feel his hard cock pressing against my core. It almost feels like an electrical shock runs through me, and I am suddenly so turned on that I feel like

I may scream if I don't have Jensen inside me immediately. I lock my legs around his waist, grinding against him as I work on the button of his jeans.

Jensen's lips travel down the side of my neck and back up, nipping and sucking; his breathing is harsh and shallow. I cry out triumphantly when I manage to get his pants undone, reaching into the opening to wrap my hand around his hard cock.

"I need this. Please." I am not above begging, but lucky for me, Jensen is more than happy to oblige. He whips my shirt off over my head before popping the clasp on my bra. When my breasts sway free, he groans before taking a hard nipple into his mouth. His hand comes up to tweak and twist my other nipple, and I can't help but grind down harder. I'm scrabbling at his shirt when he turns around and drops me onto the bed. He pulls his shirt off over his head and grabs my leggings, ripping them down my legs so that I am almost bare before him.

"Oh, my gorgeous girl. How I have missed you." Jensen kicks out of his jeans before kneeling on the ground between my open thighs. When I sit up slightly to see him, his eyes are hot and greedy as they stare at my panty-covered pussy like all the treasures of the world are there for the taking. Sliding his hands slowly up the length of my legs, Jensen maintains eye contact until he reaches the waistband of my panties, which he promptly rips in two. My body arches off the bed as he immediately buries his face in between my legs, running his tongue up and down my slit in long, wet strokes. My hands go to his hair, gripping and pulling as he tortures me with long, slow licks.

I'm a babbling mess of nerves and sensations when he nips my clit with his teeth, detonating my building orgasm with an efficiency that causes my breath to catch on a wailing scream. Jensen climbs up onto the bed between my legs and smirks at me, his lips glistening with the remnants of my orgasm.

"That was just the beginning, angel baby. I am nowhere near done with you. We have time to make up for." He latches onto my nipple again, sliding one finger in me, pumping slowly before moving up to two and then three. I can feel the stretch, and while it stings, I welcome it because I know that the next thing is his cock, and I want that buried so deep in me that we can't tell where one of us begins and the other ends.

"Please, Jensen. Please. I need you." My hands fly up to grip the comforter, and I raise my knees to lock on his hips, but Jensen grins against my nipple and bites a bit harder.

"Oh, you're going to get it, angel baby. When I give it to you, you can run this house any way you see fit, but in this bedroom or bed? I make all the rules, and I want to have a play." His fingers pump faster, and I can feel my hips rising and falling to meet him thrust for thrust. His cock is hot and hard against my inner thigh, and without thinking, I reach down and grip it hard, sliding my hand up and down his length. He groans in encouragement, and I go faster, matching his speed as his fingers slide in and out of me.

"That feels so good, angel baby. That's right, stroke your man's cock. Oh god, that feels so good. Fuck. You're going to make me come if you keep that up, and I only want to come in this tight pussy." He growls as he pulls my hand away and uses his other hand to coat his cock in my juices, staring down at me with eyes blazing with desire.

"You ready for this?" he asks, and I nod frantically because I feel like I have been ready for a million years. Jensen pulls me closer to the edge of the bed and notches himself at my entrance before slowly sliding in. I gasp and moan, bucking against him as my body stretches to accommodate his girth. "Fuck. You are so tight. Goddamn, how am I meant to last when your pussy feels this amazing?" He grips my thighs harder, fighting for control as he starts to rock back and forth, giving my body more time to adjust to his intrusion. However, I don't want to be slow and don't need time to adjust. I need Jensen to fuck me, and I need him to do it now.

"Fuck me like you mean it." His nostrils flare at the challenge before the cocky grin I love so much graces his lips.

"As you wish, angel baby. Hold on tight." He snaps his hips forward in a rough thrust that has me screaming in pleasure and begging incoherently for more. "This what you wanted, angel baby? You wanted me to use this little pussy? Make it mine again? Then again, it's always been mine, hasn't it?" Jensen leans forward and pinches a nipple, twisting roughly, and I can feel my eyes roll into the back of my head. It feels like nothing I have ever felt before and everything I have ever needed, all rolled into one.

My hands are twisting in the comforter as Jensen continues to play my body like his favorite instrument, making it sing in ways I never knew it could. I watch him lick two fingers before swirling them in circles around my clit, and I come undone immediately and without warning. Jensen praises me, telling me what a good girl I am for coming for him and how I will do it again because he needs more. I shake my head back and forth, certain there is no way I can come again so quickly.

"Oh yes, angel baby. I need one more. Give it to me. Give it to me now." He adjusts the angle of my hips and, in doing so, hits a whole new spot that, up until that moment, I never knew existed. "There it is. Do you like that? I know you do. Such a good angel baby. You'll come again for me, right? Aren't you a good girl?" Sweat covers his chest as he leans over me to press his lips to mine. I kiss him back, tasting myself on his lips but not caring. I can hear the sounds I am making. Jensen fucks me, but I am beyond caring. I can feel the tremble start in the pit of my stomach and radiate outward.

"Close. So close. Please."

Jensen slides one hand back down to my clit, teasing me with the flat of his fingers. Leaning forward, he whispers in my ear, "Come." Then he pinches my clit, and I come so hard that black specks float in front of my eyes. Jensen increases his pace, grunting as his eyes bore into mine. I'm a puddle of emotions and sensations beneath him as his rhythm starts to falter.

"Fuck. Fuck. Fuck. Fuck!" I can feel Jensen coming deep inside me in long, hot spurts, and the feeling is almost enough to make me come again. My muscles jump and quiver, but I wrap my arms around his neck and hold on tight as he rides out his orgasm, gasping harshly. When he collapses next to me on the bed, he immediately pulls me against his chest.

We lay there for what feels like hours as our heart rates return to normal and we learn how to breathe again. When I sit up to go to the bathroom and clean up, I realize I can feel him trickling out of me, and I freeze. Jensen notices my change in demeanor and sits up, trying to get me to turn and face him.

"Did I hurt you? Lily? Please, look at me. I will never forgive myself if I hurt you. Please."

I look up at him. It takes a few tries, but I finally manage to croak out, "We didn't use anything."

Chapter Forty-One

Jensen

"I know. There will never be anything between us ever again." I keep my tone and face calm as I see her starting to freak out. I tug her back down to lay against me. "I am here, in this, with you, for the long haul. Whatever happens, we will face together. Every new adventure and day will be you and me against the world." I kiss her temple, and she relaxes against me. "If you prefer that we wait before we add to our family, then we can, but I would prefer there never be anything between us again."

"I haven't thought about children before. They were part of a future I didn't think I would get to have." Lily stares out the window as she contemplates the possibilities of our new life.

"Well, now that you can, what do you think?" When she smiles at me, I know the answer.

"I would love to have kids someday, but right now, I just want to focus on you and me. Is that okay?" She bites her bottom lip, and I can't help but chuckle because she is adorable.

"That is perfectly reasonable, and I love the idea. Maybe you can even come on tour with us if we go back out." The group is in shambles, and I do not know what is happening. Grayson is spiraling, Delilah is oblivious, and last I heard, Mia is holed up with Law, her body guard, in a cabin somewhere remote.

"That could be fun. I haven't gotten to travel much outside of campaign trails. I think traveling with you might be my new favorite thing." She kisses my cheek before stealing the sheet and hopping out of bed to enter the bathroom.

"Don't think you just can skip out on finishing this house. I am not doing all of this on my own." My tone is teasing, and she leans back into the bedroom, giving me a cheeky grin.

"I would never leave this to you. You have no taste." She sticks her tongue out at me, and I jump up off the bed and manage to snag her as she tries to skate by me out the door. Picking her up, I swing her around until I can toss her lightly on the bed and cover her body with my own.

"I will have you know that I have the absolute best taste in the world!" Lily is giggling uncontrollably, and I smile back down at her as I smooth her wild curls.

"Oh, you do, do you?" I lean forward to nip at her nose.

"Of course I do. I picked you." Her blue eyes shimmer with tears as I brush my lips against her once and again before deepening the kiss. Her arms wind around my neck as she kisses me back. I tug the sheet apart as I settle in between her open thighs. Pulling back, I cup her cheek, running my thumb back and forth. "I love you so much. You know that, right?"

"I love you too." Lily runs her hand through my hair before tugging my head back down as our lips meet again. She sighs against my lips before arching her back and pressing closer to me.

"Angel baby, you're playing with fire." I know she has to be sore, so I thought we'd spend the day being lazy around the house before meeting with the family later in the evening.

"What if I want to get burned?" At her whispered words, the logical part of my brain dies quickly. Nothing matters anymore but giving my girl precisely what she is asking for.

"As you wish, angel baby." I sit back and toss her up to the head of the bed before flipping her onto her front. Slapping her ass, I lean forward and take a bite. Lily squeals, and I chuckle. "Hands and knees, angel baby. Don't make me wait." As she gets in position, I slide my hands up her inner thigh until I get to her center. Sliding a finger through her folds, it comes back dripping wet. I add another finger and pump them in and out of her as she moans in encouragement.

Grinning, I press into her, holding her hips in place as she tries to push back onto me. "No, no, no. I want to take my time." I keep my thrusts slow and steady, enjoying the feeling of being joined with her. "Can you feel how great we are together? Fuck, I love you."

Lily is panting under me, and I can't think of a sweeter sound. "Jensen, please," Lily whines.

"Please, what? Do you want me to speed up? Slow down? Tell me what you need, angel baby." When she tries to push back against me again, I smack a hand down on her ass, appreciating the pale pink her skin turns.

"I need you to move. I need more. I don't know. I just need more." Her irritation is adorable, and I can't help but grin, knowing that she can't see my face.

"As you wish, angel baby." I slap my hips forward in a rough thrust that has her head flying up, causing her curls to fall in a mass down her back. "You are so gorgeous. I can't wait to make you my wife."

"Who said I was gonna marry you?" Lily snarks back.

"Your left hand." Lily gasps as she looks down at the ring I snuck onto her hand while wrestling her into position. I don't give her time to overthink it. I adjust my angle, hitting that spot she loves and sliding my hand around to the front to swirl around her clit. She immediately falls apart under me, and I can't help it; my rhythm falters, and I fall over the edge after her. I roll us until she is on top of me while trying to catch my breath.

"Mark my words, Lily Grace DuPont. You are going to marry me. I won't hear anything else on the matter."

We're both still trying to catch our breath, but I hear her whisper, "About time."

"You know we'll have to see the family, right?" We're sitting under our tree in the afternoon sun. Weather in Texas this time of year is a sunny sixty with a constant breeze. It's the best time of the year. Lily tenses from where she was lounging in between my legs.

"Do we have to?"

I can hear the worry in her voice, and I turn her to face me. "What are you worried about?" Lily refuses to meet my eyes. That doesn't work for me, so I tilt her face to mine. "Angel baby? I'm not ashamed of our relationship. Are you?"

"No! Never! I just worry about what they will say."

I turn her around so that we're face to face. "Lily. I need you to listen to me, okay? They are gone if they are anything other than happy for us. Cut out of our lives. With that being said, the only people that belong in our life are those in our corner. I am not worried. Our parents love us, and our happiness matters to them."

Lily sighs before sitting back down against me. "Okay. We can go."

I smile as I kiss the top of her head. "Lily, it's just dinner, not the guillotine. It will be okay. I promise. Also, I'm glad you agreed because we are meeting them for dinner at six." She hits me in the shoulder, but it lacks any heat. I laugh and pull her closer as we stare out over the field

me in the shoulder, but it lacks any heat. I laugh and pull her closer as we stare out over the field

Chapter Forty Two

Lily

Walking into the Parker house, cheers greet me as everyone rises to hug us, passing us from one family member to the next. In the short time I've been gone, I almost forgot how loud and lively they are. When I return to Jensen, we stand before our parents, who are both grinning.

"You're finally home!" Michael hugs me, and Jensen thumps him on the back.

Mom pulls me close. "My girl, I've missed you."

I hug her tightly. "We're free, Mom."

Tears well in my eyes as she holds me tighter. "I tried so hard, but in the end, I just—"

I stop her with a smile. "I know. I get it now. That's the past. All I care about is the life we're going to build."

I glance back at Jensen and smile. Mom notices the ring on my finger. "Mike! He did it! He did it!" A cheer erupts, startling me.

Jensen laughs as Mike grabs me, spinning me around. "It's about time! Let me see!" He admires the ring, and I still can't believe no one is upset.

"You're not mad?" I look back and forth between our parents, but both are beaming.

"Mad? Heavens no! We've been waiting for this for years!" Mom says, and I can't help but feel confused.

"Years?"

Mike chuckles. "You two weren't as discreet in high school as you thought. After school, I worried—Jensen went off the rails, and you were stuck with that sorry sack of shit who called himself a father. All we could do was hope things would work out, and here you are! Our prayers answered!"

Jensen pulls me close as the Parker clan surrounds us. "We need a party! ¡Ándale! Let's go!" Abuela says and ushers everyone outside, and I'm stunned to see the uncles and cousins setting up tables and chairs on the lawn. Someone's rigging up a sound system, grills are being prepared. The love and acceptance overwhelm me, and I can't stop smiling, even as tears threaten to spill.

"Angel baby, you okay?" Of course Jensen notices, always attuned to my emotions. I laugh as I see neighbors crossing the street and Alexander and Delilah pulling up.

"For the first time in a long time, I think I am." I hug him, and we head down the steps to join our family.

One Year Later

A year to the day from that porch moment, we said our vows beneath our tree in a small, intimate ceremony. My tea-length dress was simple yet elegant. Alexander walked me down the aisle. Delilah stood by my side as maid of honor, and Mike, newly officiated, led the ceremony. I danced with Mike for the father-daughter dance, and Jensen swayed with Mom, bringing her to tears.

It was perfect.

From the Author

For a free bonus epilogue to This is Meant to Be, giving you a snapshot of Jensen and Lily in the future, follow this link: https://dl.bookfunnel.com/n5a2nps4ub

Thank you so much for reading This is Meant to Be. If you have a moment, please leave a review: they are unbelievably important to the books' success and are greatly appreciated. Are you ready for Grayson and Maddie's story? They will be coming your way in 2025! Check my Facebook group for preorder information! Want to know more about Delilah and Alexander? Check out their book This is Growing Up while you wait!

SmutTok Made Me Do It Facebook Group

Juliet McKinleys Book Nook

Sign Up for my newsletter here so that you never miss a beat, giveaway or sneak peek-

Newsletter   julietmckinley.myflodesk.com

TikTok   @JulieyMcKinleyAuthor

Instagram   @JulietMckinleyAuthor

Facebook   Juliet McKinley